The Planet Suite

♀♀⊕♂♃♄♅♆♇

Allen Ashley

EibonVale
www.eibonvalepress.co.uk

Acknowledgements

"Seven Rides To Venus" originally published in "The Third Alternative 3"

"Cosmic Scrapbook" originally published as a mini chapbook given away with "The Third Alternative" (1997)

"The Perils of Pentavir" originally published in "Dark Horizons 51"

"That First Book Feeling" originally published in "Zene issue 9"

"Spaced Out in the Slipstream" originally published in "Dragon's Breath 46/47"

"The Astronauts" originally published in "Hawkfrendz Winter 88"

"Music from The Spheres" is published here for the first time.

Allen Ashley is a British Fantasy Award winner with 13 books to his name as author or editor. These include "Creeping Crawlers" (as editor, Shadow Publishing) and "Dreaming Spheres: Poems of the Solar System" (with Sarah Doyle, PS Publishing). This is his fourth book with Eibonvale Press. He works as a creative writing tutor and also as a critical reader for an agency.

Contents:

Seven Rides to Venus

Only Skin Deep

We had expected a cloud-enshrouded world of poisoned gas but instead we landed on a desert plain. The sand was swept into lusciously curving dunes that rolled with the undulating contours of healthy skin. The air was clear, warm with pastel whites and yellows. The sand was light brown and inviting to the touch. We removed our gloves and let our hands run over it, or dribbled the soft grains through our fingers. We were content for hours to merely caress the landscape.

At home we had passed two million years as parasites destroying our hostess. The perfect skin of Venus gave us a second chance to learn to live as caring symbiotes.

Those of us not smitten into total immobility explored a little further over the crest of the gentle hill. Silicon stretched out in every direction, broken in several areas by small pools of salty water surrounded by spidery fronds of a grass strain new to us.

Over time our instruments detected a regular rising and falling of the surface level. But we did not fear seismic eruptions. Rather, we realised that the Gaeans were correct, that each planet, sun, star and any other heavenly body was a living entity. We only regretted the necessity of travelling twenty five million miles to make such an obvious deduction.

*

Eye of the Beholder

Dutch Uncle Nicholas had often delighted in telling the children that the first nocturnal object to rise, the so-called 'evening star', was in fact the planet Venus.

Jane thought of it as a hot, tropical world full of green plants like the Great Palm House at Kew. Eddie insisted it was all deserts and gases.

In high summer they slept up in the loft with the skylight open. Eddie had a telescope and sometimes let his sister play with it, making it expand and contract. But he interfered too much as well.

"Stop it, you're making my eye hurt!" she would shout.

"You'll have to scream louder than that, girlie, to attract the attention of those two Venus-worshippers downstairs."

She thought she knew what he meant. She wasn't quite sure. Her brother had gone a little strange recently. He bunked off school to get home early in the afternoon and watch 18-certificate videos. He sat up late with their astronomer uncle talking nonchalantly about orbital probes and whether space was one big hole or a Swiss cheese.

"Come on, Jane, what can you see? Any flashes of lightning yet?"

"White ... brown ... red ... don't push so, it's painful! Yes, now silver ... silver ... I can't blink it away."

"Yeah, told you so."

He was off to the other side of the room ... mercifully. How old did they have to be before their parents let them have separate bedrooms?

The world had wobbled several times during its rotation of late. Mum and Dad had acrimoniously split up three years ago. Jane had taken it badly and had made a point of studiously sticking pins into a doll until her teacher had suggested there might be several sides to every story. So Jane had then washed the doll with her own tears and, miracle of miracles, their mother and father were now attempting a romantic reconciliation. To a large degree childcare had gone out of the window as the couple rediscovered the pleasure of each other's celestial body.

Jane had spent a long time crouched against the keyhole observing their starlit couplings. Her big brother knew this and her eyes were made to pay the price for their inquisitiveness.

Everything was a little strange recently. It was all Jane could do to keep her grades up at school.

The Way Back to the Womb

How strange this place with its mismatched rotation and orbital periods, this planet where a day is longer than a year. We stick to the twilight area, moving with the slowness of mule-less nomads through the dense jungle. The humidity is like a drug, making us at once lethargic and yet sexually aroused. Our declared mission is to locate the purple valley espied by our space telescopes, but instead my colleagues regularly digress into the thick undergrowth to make the beast with two backs. I am as primed as they are. Jane, the focus of my affections, has lately been in a work detail separate from her husband. She talks with me, touches my arm, and looks at me with direct green eyes. The aphrodisiac jungle draws us inexorably closer together.

The captain has told us not to remove our protective suits but many have been lax about such things. Back home they told us lies about unbearable temperatures and poisonous gases. There is a touch more carbon dioxide, it's true, but it only serves to make the plants grow thicker. Sometimes they are an impenetrable screen. This is how the rainforests must have been once upon a time on Earth. I only hope the loggers are not immediately behind us. We must protect Venus from their rape and pillage.

My love and I are thrown together in the effort and the perspiration of mapping the virgin territory all around us. We explore each other concurrently. We are wet ... sticky ... intertwined.

I heard a theory somewhere that each planet in the solar system is at a different stage of its life cycle – the further from the sun, the more advanced towards eventual decay. Thus, masculine Mars lies wretched and war-torn, its soil the colour of dried blood. Earth teeters on the brink, a diseased blue and white marble. Venus, however, is the new Garden of Eden: verdant and moist, the legitimate target of our explorations and probing.

There are serpents in the rivers that form the delta. The ground is lush. There is much fruit to pluck.

Sniff This

The Bank Holiday Fair drew crowds of young people from all the local towns and villages. It was the only place where one could meet a different bunch of fellers. Why then, Jane reflected, did she still seem to be lumbered with her brother Eddie and his best friend Jack?

Never mind, she loved fairs. The jewel strings of flashing lights, the smooth patter of the barkers, the mud and the wheel tracks, the distorted disco music blaring out from each separate attraction. And that was not all. You could close your eyes and cover your ears so as to experience an olfactory assault: machine oil, fried onions, burnt burgers, girls with perfume, candy floss and toffee apples, the harsh smell of electric sparks from the dodgem platform...

Eddie was tugging her arm.

"Come on, we're going on this ride. I'll pay."

It was called *Voyage to Venus*. The car – or more correctly, capsule – shot straight up and then rotated in ecstatic circles amid a plethora of pulsing lights and tunes that faded in and out like a decaying transistor. When they came back to earth she felt quite disorientated, unable to stand or even see properly, assailed by the odours from the hot dog stand nearby. If that was space travel no wonder the Americans had all but abandoned it.

This time it was Jack pulling at her wrist. A stranger would have received a slap but Jack was almost family. He guided her over to some sort of haunted house. Jane didn't see what it was called. Just glorified lorries, anyway.

Inside, it smelled like a butcher's shop. She retched but didn't produce. She wanted to come out again, tried to turn but the floor was slippery and the walls were wet and slightly furry to the touch. Probably best just to carry on, get the torture over with. She took a few tentative steps. Then a few more. It must be a deep trailer. Shouldn't she have to turn at a right angle very soon? But no, the route was straight ahead and upward slightly.

She could hear no one behind her and only assumed the lads were ahead. The walls of what she now took to be a tunnel were moving inexorably closer together. Supposing the whole thing came to a dead end? Supposing it was a really tight squeeze and they all had to clamber out backwards?

The place was becoming both stinkier and increasingly airless. She was inhaling as if she was on a mountain climb and the combined smell of blood, pus, flesh and mucus was a veritable assault on the senses. There was nothing to see and nothing to hear. She could only smell, touch or, God forbid, taste!

How much longer? She was suffocating. The experience was more than uncomfortable.

Then she could just about see Jack in front of her. He was making rapid circular motions with his pointed head. *He'd* set her up for this. She could barely breathe. To inhale would only cause further distress.

The solution was simple now she thought of it.

She gave a huge snort, exhaling, freeing herself from all nasal obstruction, out in the fresh air again, on the wet grass, laughing at her friend's disarranged clothes and the audacity of their orificial explorations.

Foaming at the Mouth

Human customs meant that some of the scientific samples collected on the first flight to Venus were retained as diplomatic gifts to friendly countries. One such publicly bestowed present went to the female head of a royal family in a decaying Old World nation. The Garden of Eden bloom had a long, thick stalk topped by a curved grouping of sensitive petals. It looked a little like a tulip and a lot like a circumcised penis. Careless of the cameras, the princess expressed her delight by kissing the protruding bud and then, like an enormous queen bee, commenced sucking at the succulent nectar.

Space flowers immediately became the *de rigueur* accoutrement, and indeed pastime, of the rich and idle. No afternoon was complete without a blow on the bloom.

Jane Wylie, a member of the original landing party, casually suggested on TV that with Earth's increasing levels of greenhouse gases and rising temperatures the Venusian flora might well grow in the average back garden. Paradise beckoned. Very soon packets of space seeds were openly available at fairs and markets across the globe. The plant proved to be a hardy little beast, choking off the competitive wheat, grass, rice and potato strains with the agility of dandelions and the ferocity of the Boston strangler.

The nectar was variously described as sweet, milky or salty. Several eminent scientists professed its nutritious value. All confessed to its slightly narcotic and somewhat addictive nature. Governments and churches passed hasty laws and edicts against this oral gratification but they were impossible rules to enforce when anyone could clamber over the railings of their local park and indulge themselves at leisure.

Commerce, production and the once frantic exchange of information tailed off into almost nothingness as the world's population sought only to fulfil themselves with the phallic flowers. The long dreamed of return to a simpler, pastoral society seemed imminent.

Overindulged and slightly immune to the spitting tulip, a gang of ruffians broke into the National Space Laboratories, Nevada. They were convinced that the manned expedition had brought back further treasures, maybe something of a potency beyond the drug currently holding the world in thrall.

Security was lax. The mostly female lab assistants and technicians sat around enjoying the cone of delights brought back from the second planet. They smiled at the intruders and waved them into the back rooms.

At length, the men found what they thought they were looking for. Not entirely without education, they realised that even plants can have a masculine and a feminine form. The so-called *space flower* was clearly the former and here inside an unlocked glass case lay what was seemingly its companion. Red, widely spread petals beckoned with the promise of muscular moistness. The *labia veneria* was like a more rounded, approachable version of its earthly but Venus-named cousin, the flytrap. Trousers and underpants were dispensed with. One guy was heard to mutter, "Is this wise?" but most males would admit to being led by their penis. The salivating mouths were waiting.

A combined scream rent the air, disturbing the engorged reverie of the workers in other areas of the complex. A death gargle became intelligible words.

"Holy shit, man! These things have got *teeth*!"

Anal Retention

Our gang leader Eddie had taken to passing a series of pornographic photos around the classroom. They were back views only. I became obsessed with one shot of long, thin white buttocks promising much devilment between them. Eddie caught my mood and upped the price several hundred per cent. I swore and haggled but paid up.

He made a lascivious, clucking sound with his tongue and said, "It's not much to pay for the rear side of Venus, is it?"

Jack, my other best friend, snorted. "I thought it was Helen of Troy ... the arse that launched a thousand shits!"

His crudity didn't bother me. I had dreams, fantasies. I knew where I was going.

We liked English Lit. but preferred it *au naturel*, so we bunked off for the afternoon.

Then we were in The Wastelands. Our parents didn't approve – they never had. It was terminally dangerous. Only the bravest boys and a few hardly girls dared.

At one end of the forgotten valley was a river of sludge. On a hot day you could smell it ten furlongs away and in close proximity the Geiger counter on my wrist would tick itself hoarse. It was best to stay up on the high ground. I kept my boots on for rock climbing.

Summer had made children of us all and we played an epic game of hide and seek, discovering ever more obscure nooks and crannies in which to lie undetected for apparent hours.

There was a girl on our team whom I'd adored for all eternity. Jane Wylie.

Back at the bike sheds she'd told me, "I know what you want, Simon, and just this once I want it too. I want you standing behind me, your hands on my breasts, your body pressed against me, your penis rubbing against my backside."

Such explicit promises! But first there was always the chase. She was pretty and smiling from the front, white skinned with black hair. She turned and raced off ahead. Seen from the rear, she was the very likeness of the goddess in the photo. I followed till she vanished into a fissure in the rocks.

The sky was darkening. I pushed and shoved and tried to force my way in but my progress was only partial. There must have been some occult trick to it, some open sesame that I had yet to learn.

Without warning, the never-dormant volcanoes of the region woke to full activity, spewing out gas and lava in all directions. I redoubled my efforts, pushing harder and faster. My friends and the game were forgotten. There was, as ever, only one goal.

And no turning back. The ground was tearing apart even as I breathed the musky air. I could feel a slow rumbling under the surface, like a train coming ... the volcanoes and geysers were red and yellow ... behind my eyelids only white-burned spots ... a rumbling like a train ... coming ... like a train ... the luckless cavern ... the spewing hot liqueous gases ... and my friends ... boys and girls together ... apart ... imaginary ... all taken by the earthquake ... the decaying mountains ... the heat of Venus.

It was dangerous to play in The Wastelands. My parents and teachers had always said so. One day we might die from it.

*

Ear to the Ground

Dutch Uncle Nicholas had some news for us. He sat us one upon each knee, Jane Wylie and I, although really we were getting a bit old for such treats. He'd become a Professor of Astronomy at the age of nineteen, having formulated a revolutionary theory about planetary positions and the history of the solar system.

Now, however: "I've had to resign," he told us. "You see, I've changed my opinions. We are the centre of the bubble. Everything else is just illusion, distortions caused by the surface tension on the inner skin."

Mother came in and told us to run along and play or she'd box our ears. Aren't we ever allowed to grow up? I took Jane by the hand and we skipped off to the beach to collect whelks and scallops. I felt sorry for my uncle. I found it easy to believe in contradictory things. At school we were expected to swallow both religion and evolution as if our ears were mere receptacles with no sense of discrimination.

None of the shells contained a goddess using her long red hair to preserve her modesty. Still, when Jane was with me I didn't need any goddesses. I held a shell and listened to the echoing rush of my bloodstream. The gently crashing sea kept time with my pounding heart. We undressed and swam for a while before continuing our holiday project on voyages to Venus. There was a spiral route I had to take but the entrance to the hole was too small, as we'd known it would be. Her white lobes were soft, minutely pierced. I was stained with golden wax. The waves washed us clean.

At sunset we walked away from the town lights along to the western cliff in order to watch the stars rise. We made a wish on sighting the yellow evening star, knowing of course that it was really the planet Venus, site of three successful excursions ... or should that read incursions?

Every society renames the constellations. Until the intrusive Galileo pointed his telescope at it, the Milky Way was the flow from the breast of Hera, mother of warriors.

Or maybe it's semen dripping back out of the orifices in the sky.

A mile inland, the radio astronomers are listening to the history of the stars. A succession of stories of flight and departure. Everything is moving away from us. We begin in unison but are sent into inevitable orbit. Jane was with me but now is gone.

The sea is crashing onto the shells like blood and bodily fluids onto the bones of the inner ear. The Earth shuddered ever so slightly in its diurnal rotation. I'm surprised they didn't mention it on the news.

All actions are an attempt to catch up with and reclaim the echoes and the substance of everything that sped away from us at the moment of creation.

We must make ready to ride to Venus again.

Jupiter – and Beyond

4

It was hard to tell whether this was A-Level History or English, especially as Mr Holkham, old Hocus-Pocus, taught Geography as well and was regularly prone to wild philosophical diversions.

"I would have been a scientist, you know, but never quite managed the empirical discipline. Me? Failing on discipline!"

Jane looked across at Simon and smiled as they simultaneously put their pens down on their desk-rests. Eddie continued to bait their master.

"I always thought Isaac Newton was eighteenth or nineteenth century," he opined.

"1642 to 1727," reeled off their teacher.

"So you're saying that Newton formulating his Law of Gravitation in 1666 is somehow connected to the Great Fire of London?"

"Indubitably. Everything must come *down*. Everything must burn *down*."

"You should meet my Uncle Nicholas," Eddie suggested and the rest of the class giggled. "Two fruits make a pair," he added sub-vocally.

"So you keep saying. Doubtless I will. All things must come to pass in an infinite universe. Talking of which," – Holkham pulled an affectatious fob watch out of his waistcoat – "I believe we have some celestial theory to catch up on at the beach."

To mixed groans and muffled cheers he led his teenage charges off premises and through town to the eternal sand and shingle. Two opportunists quit on the way but Jack was there with the fags; also Alison the fashion victim; Joe, Linda, Phil and Bill; Rebecca with a half-full hip flask of vodka; and Simon who'd stopped off on the way to load up with two bottles of cider from the offy where they never asked your age. And Jane. Always Jane.

"The stars, my young friends," the professor began without further ado, "are as numberless as the grains of sand on a beach. I believe William Blake said something to that effect."

"He was a fruitcake, too," muttered Simon.

"Now then," continued Hocus-Pocus, asteroid sized eyes bulging behind his specs, "I suggest for our extracurricular project we indeed begin to count the number of grains on this Shiplea beach."

Affected American accent from Joe: "You cannot be serious!"

"I certainly can. Do you want to stay on for a second year or are you going to drop out like your chum ... David, wasn't it?"

"Beyond," all corrected.

"Beg your pardon?"

"Beyond," said Jane. "It's what everyone calls him now."

"Hmm. Interesting moniker. Serves to remind us that every stone is but an echo of the first explosion. Matter and energy are still being carried outwards. The tide doesn't just break here, it ripples outwards in every conceivable direction." Eddie was making screw-loose gestures. Holkham chose to ignore him, turned to Simon and said, "You there, what's yer name?"

"Simon, sir."

"Simon-sir, what do you think you'd find if you were able to look right across this sea to the other side?"

"I don't know. Holland? Denmark?"

"No, young man, you'd be looking right back at the primal moment, the jolly old Big Bang. Think on that, if you will. And in the meantime, give me a sip of that cider. It's thirsty work counting the stars."

"Especially in the daytime," suggested Jack.

Linda and Alison went swimming in their school clothes, emerged to the cheers of the boys with their skirts plastered high up their thighs and their white shirts revealing rounded mermaid breasts spiked by visible nipples. Eddie and Phil indulged in an arduous bout of arm wrestling before pestering the girls for an opportunity to dry their glistening skin with the rough worsted of their Shiplea High blazers. Jack cadged a light off an old dear with a Dalmatian and when he'd ground the dog-end into the silicon he tapped his watch and politely informed the pipe-smoking lecturer that it was 'home time'.

"So go home, then," waved Hocus-Pocus airily as he resumed his contemplation on subjects greater than the earning of a daily crust.

Simon sat with Jane, saying very little, occasionally attempting an estimate of the granular composition of a square inch, which could be luxuriously multiplied… if he hadn't left his calculator back in the sixth form locker area.

"That guy gives astronomy a bad name," stated Simon after a half-hour or so.

"That guy gives wacky baccy a bad name," Jane replied, giggling.

As the sun set into the sea like a round of red liver squashed onto a butcher's slab, the early stars broke through the blue shroud. Simon felt he ought to offer to buy Jane a coke or something but the trip to the off-licence had cleaned him out. They sat close by but not touching, looking alternately at the dregs of spit and cider coagulating in the bottom of the bottle and up to the increasingly speckled heavens.

"Is that one Jupiter or Venus?" she asked.

"I'm not sure. I'd have to check my maps."

She could not mask her disappointment. "I thought you knew all these things."

"I forget. I don't practise enough. It's like anything else."

She rose unsteadily. "I'm going home. See you for French tomorrow. Sweet dreams about me."

If only you knew, he thought. Hands … knee tremblers … and boomps a daisy! Another Big Bang becomes a damp squib.

*

We have been hovering around Jupiter for two days now. The gas giant taunts us: Come closer, fall into my methane seas, swim in my mobile skin.

I paid a secret visit to the ship's doctor this morning. He has diagnosed an advanced case of solipsism.

"Not uncommon on space flights," he opined; but what does he know? The universe did not exist before the moment of my birth. It was held in a state of readiness at my conception and may yet be confined to the limbo of history unless I can get our delicious captain, Jane Wylie, to start sharing my contour couch.

The physician gave me some tablets but I do not trust any drugs. Just occasionally I succumb to painkillers for the blinding headaches which blight my adulthood. However, I crushed his prescription pills into yellow-white powder and fed them into the waste disposal. As everything is recycled, we may all get to suffer their mild side effects of microdot hallucinations.

I am in two minds about the giant gonad dominating our view screen, In truth, I remember more spectacular cloud patterns accompanying the sun setting into the sea at Shiplea when I was a child. And yet there is an undoubted fascination in the extraordinarily precise and symmetrical colour arrangements of the boss planet. Yesterday I set my PC to reconfiguring these patterns into meaningful text or images but so far the computer has only come up with abstract drivel or gibberish.

We are all looking for an answer. Rumours persist that there is some sort of barrier encapsulating the solar system and that all data apparently from outside is mere surface distortion on the inner skin. In effect, we are inside a huge bubble. I don't subscribe to the theory myself but this quasi-religious view has swept through the better brains of Earth like a virus. We can only speculate. It is not our mission.

Yet.

*

She'd been watching a wagtail on the lawn for several minutes but her sudden repositioning at the kitchen window had sent the hungry bird skittering into the air. Jane went back to her bedroom to carry on with her literature revision but -

"What are you two doing in here?"

It was Eddie – Jupiter, as he now styled himself – and his dopey sidekick Beyond.

"That play you were in last year," Eddie replied. "We thought you might still have some stage make-up."

"All the world's a stage," added Beyond.

"Well you might at least have asked me first," Jane answered. "Anyway, what do you two want with make-up? You've not gone ducky, have you?"

She thought for a moment that her brother was going to hit her. She could hear him grinding his teeth, counting to ten before pulling something from the inside pocket of his beaten-up black coat. It was a photo of some Norfolk fishermen, taken fifty, maybe even eighty years ago.

"I got the idea from Clockwork Orange," Eddie stated. "Thought we needed a group identity, a gang look, right? But until I can grow bushy sideburns like old Henry Bollock here I've got to make do and mend, ain't I?"

She shook her head in amazement. "I never knew you were so well up on local history," she commented. "I haven't got any stage make-up or sideburns," she added. "Why can't you just make do with leather jackets like all the other tough kids?"

Eddie pushed past her. "That's a stupid question," he snapped.

Beyond followed in his wake. "Was God an astronaut?" he mumbled. "Now that's a good question."

*

The numerologists were still having a field day. Academic doubts cast on the absolute accuracy of ancient calendars meant they could keep the whole wild charabanc going for a decade or more. Prophets a-plenty came to prominence. There was virtue, there was abstinence, there was piety. There was also self-aggrandisement, power and hypocrisy. In other areas – the much-maligned inner cities, for example – there was unbridled hedonism of an intensity never before witnessed. World society was taking two different directions at once: rioting and penance; orgies and pilgrimages. What kind of place were we passing on to future generations? And who cared, anyhow?

Governments pondered. Governments pandered. Governments and pan-national interest groups took direct action or closed up shop and sought to save their own skins for when the crisis blew over. The whole terracotta terran pot came closer to the boil.

Shielded somewhat from the emotional roller coaster afflicting most of Earth, a scientific community in the northern hinterlands of Scandinavia made a disturbing discovery. There was much double-checking and a veritable flurry of coded cross-references with other European, American and Asian bases. The Finnish astronomers took care to gain collateral confirmation without revealing their results.

Their conclusion was that in just three years, three months and twenty-one days' time all nine planets of the solar system would be in an arrow-straight line pointing directly at the sun. Rather like a selection of coloured balls on a three- dimensional snooker table waiting for the huge, glowing cue ball to pot the lot of them. Or swallow them all whole...

Wasn't nine the holy Islamic number? Didn't the Chinese speak of an ultimate balance between yin and yang? Wasn't an impending Day of Judgement at the back of everyone's mind whether they were on their knees praying or drugged-up to the eyeballs and partying? If word got out...

The odds against Sol and his children becoming aligned in this way were calculated at four point six billion to one, which, by a numbing coincidence, was the approximate age in years of the solar system. The debate would soon rage as to whether the whole of creation was simply a mathematical experiment set in motion by either chance or a Supreme Being. The cosmic gyroscope seemed now to be spinning inexorably towards its predetermined conclusion. Computers sifted through all available historical data. Their revelations appeared to confirm that earlier near-misses – five, six, seven planets in a row – coincided with events such as The Great Flood, the end of the Age of Reptiles and even the first recorded appearance of algae and single-celled bacteria. For no apparent reason the old 1960s ditty about the moon being in the seventh house began to be played regularly on all the world's cable and radio stations.

Then word got out.

The die-hard hedonists died hard but the rest of the masses listened up. By now there were scarcely two and a half ordinary years in which to make amends for two and a half million years of human foul-ups. The wheels of industry ground to a halt. The labourers in the fields sheathed their scythes. The dormant food mountains of the affluent West finally found a purpose in sustaining the saints and seers of the apocalyptic conversion. There was much keening and whining, there were renewed outbreaks of self-flagellation, there were even several attempts to pass camels through the eyes of needles.

Kazuo Takiname, inventor of The Absolute Bit and second richest man in the world, was not going to sit around awaiting the fate of his ancestors. With what little workforce still believed in the twin pursuit of excellence and the yen, he had an interstellar spaceship constructed. He took with him a handpicked harem and an intelligent but obedient crew. With good luck and a prevailing solar wind they would be out beyond Halley's Comet before Judgement Day. The explosive launch of his craft from its secret base was reckoned by many to be just another seismic eruption in a sequence of surface disturbances troubling the dying planet. Francis Randolph del Amitri Smith, however, was concerned that the usual communications channels with his deadly rival were no longer open.

Del Amitri Smith was the richest person in the world. He was a man of action. When his partner Alfie Leadbetter had invented the Super-Enabler, del Amitri Smith had quietly arranged to have his friend disposed of and had taken the credit and the exponential flood of dollars for himself. Reacting to his Catholic background, Smith was sometimes privately heard to proclaim that he was bigger than Jesus and of far more significance in the Earth's long history. He wasn't just going to sit on his butt and wait till we all tipped back into the sun, no sir!

J-Day arrived and the world's population gathered to stand on tiptoe in the vain hope of seeing the love planet and the messenger sphere ahead of them whilst casting anxious glances over their shoulders, fearful that the red warlike one was about to descend on them at any second. They waited. The Universe paused. The alignment was coming together just about ... now!

Mercury erupted into a ball of flame but it was nothing to do with the sun engulfing it. Molecular disrupter missiles exploded in the gas clouds of Jupiter, pushing it ever so slightly out of orbit and creating a companion to its original scarlet spot. The weapons targeted at Neptune and Uranus failed to ignite but Pluto and its companion planet Charon were blown right out of the ether.

This last detonation also destroyed Takiname's escape ship although few realised this at the time.

Some acclaimed del Amitri Smith as a saviour. J-Day passed, and a second and a third turning, and there was no divine intervention. Maybe God had never intended to come back, but we wouldn't know for certain, now, would we?

A tide of anger and disappointment swept across the globe as billions realised that life would pretty much go on as before. They had to satisfy their bloodlust. They had to have their judgement. All the money and the fortresses and the security guards in the civilised world could not ultimately save del Amitri Smith. Thus do we treat our heroes.

Life went on pretty much as before.

*

Idle afternoons. The dull comfort and the thin cloud of tedium of a solidly middle class marriage. The open window brings the chill breeze and the threat of rain but also the susurration of the sea, the womb of life. Sometimes the tide brings memories on its crest. Sometimes she wonders if there are certain people she has known for all time, a coterie of friends with whom she'd been Ancient Britons and primordial apes and megalosauri and ammonites and reused atoms all the way back to Moment One.

"Mummy, can I go out to play?"

It took Jane a few seconds to realise that it was her own younger voice inquiring. You dream long enough of your childhood, you might just travel back there…

"All right, darling, but keep your sandals on."

"Yes, Mummy. Be back for tea."

This was when they'd lived close to the shell beach. Her friends and Dutch Uncle Nicholas were in a daisy chain around her door. They raised a ragged cheer as Jane emerged, then it was scampering feet and last one in the sea's a squashed jellyfish.

Jack was as wild as ever, swimming right out over the brown waves in his school shorts and printed shirt. Eddie would be sorry he'd missed this for a fishing trip with Father. There was lots of splashing and paddling. Her dress was wet and her sandals soaked. Dutch Uncle Nicholas took them off her feet; singing a nonsense version of This Little Piggy and letting his fingers linger rather too long on her white ankles. He placed her shoes on a rock to dry in the sunlight. It was one of those strange days when the moon is visible in the diurnal sky. The professor took pencil and notebook from his trouser pocket and settled down to some serious sketching.

The others were involved in a complicated make-believe about aliens stealing the lunar reflection and now Doctor Who and the Earthmen had to fight them to get it back. It looked rather rough and she didn't fancy spending two hours mostly screaming in the role of one of the Time Lord's assistants. Instead, she collected some seagull feathers and began a floating experiment in a shallow depression just back from the tide-line. Later she settled down to contemplate the horizon.

And now here was Simon, looking seventeen as always, accidentally shadowing the afternoon sunlight and causing her to shiver. How come in this warped memory he was now ten years older than she was? But not to worry.

"What's that you're holding, Si?"

"It's a conch shell."

"You don't find them on this beach."

"I know, Jane. Someone must have bought it in the souvenir shop and dropped it. Have a listen."

"Hmm. I can hear the sea. In my covered ear and my open ear."

"It's not the sea."

"No, it's not. Miss at school said that it's your bloodstream rushing around inside your head."

"It's not that, either," he insisted. "Dutch Uncle Nicholas explained that what you hear are the echoes of the Big Bang."

She remembered her mother telling her that Dutch Uncle Nicholas had been placed under permanent house arrest for astronomical heresy. Which placed him alongside Galileo in the great pantheon. And yet she could still see him over to the left playing "one knee down" with the boys… but you always must believe your mother.

"Right person, wrong crime," was Mummy's opinion.

"He was always very nice to us. Alison didn't like him, though."

"Yes, well, darling, he won't be bothering you little ones any more."

"I feel sad for him."

"Well don't. He wasn't Dutch and he wasn't your uncle, either."

*

The truly important events in the history of the Universe occurred during the first three minutes – yea, not even seven days – and it is our curse to be living in the endless afterthought.

If we accept the Big Bang theory then it seems likely that at some point billions of years into the future the entropic expansion will reach its limit and the Universe will start to contract. From that moment time will run backwards, so I can sit here now and picture a future occasion where all my actions will be reversed and I will systematically undo all the harm I've ever done and even eventually return to the primal innocence of the womb, the sperm penetrating – or is it withdrawing from? – the egg, the delicate twinkle in my father's eye ... and then blinked out ... forever.

Jane's pushbike skidded to a rather clumsy halt. She leaned it against a roadside beech, not bothering to lock the back wheel. There on the other side of the tarmac was the motorcycle and sidecar she had hoped to find. The two youths would be somewhere beyond the bushes in this flat East Anglian countryside. She remembered this spot from family picnics a few years back. No doubt the pair of drugged-up bikers intended to defile it in some way. I mean, it was one thing swigging a couple of bottles of cider on the school playing fields or passing a joint round during the star gate sequence of *2001*, but whatever Eddie was taking now only amplified his ordinary aggression. She pushed through some ferns and low branches, hearing giggling up ahead and feeling her T-shirt sticking wetly to her shoulder blades. He'd changed his name to Jupiter, got his chest tattooed with naked women and started picking fights in pubs. At least it meant he wasn't there pushing his year younger sister around all the time. And as for his friend Dave – 'Beyond' – he was so far gone he was probably going to boomerang right back round the curve of the Earth one of these days.

She came into a clearing. A few yards in front of her the two youths stood facing east, their black leather jackets catching the afternoon sunlight, their dirty blue jeans around their ankles, pimply white arses mooning at her startled green eyes. Were they urinating? No, their hands were moving too swiftly, they were -

"Oh my God!" she inhaled.

"Piss off, Jane!" Eddie shouted without turning round. "You're spoiling the wanking competition."

Her errant legs carried her two steps closer. "You're ... oh no, not into our special pond," she moaned.

"We're seeding the galaxy. We're boldly going where no man has before," Beyond mumbled.

"You're not men!" she screeched but maintained her distance.

"Shut the fuck up!" Jupiter ordered. "Shut up or we'll drag you into it. Is that what you want?"

Before she could reply, Beyond was asking, "Hey, Jupe, what came first, the sperm or the egg?"

"The sperm, of course, you nancy boy. Ooh ... oh yes! Beat that, you Willie Wonka!"

Jane turned away to examine the seeds on a strand of rye grass. Doubtless, they were better left alone to go hang by their own petards.

After a time, Eddie turned to face her. Mercifully flaccid amid a gorse of russet hair, he still reminded her too much of her beloved father. She spat contemptuously on the ground in front of her, a witchly habit she'd picked up from Wild Rachel. She ignored the two teenagers as they got dressed again.

Beyond was looking at something white and sticky on his right hand which wouldn't wipe off easily on the clumps of grass at his feet. He stated, "Did you know God is dog backwards?"

"Shit, everybody knows that," Eddie answered.

"And," Beyond continued, "the ... uh, reverse of mood is doom?"

"Zip it up," Eddie/Jupiter insisted. Then to his sister, "What are you doing here, anyway, out on the edge of Jodrell Bank?"

"Mother sent me. She got a letter from old Hocus-Pocus."

"That wanker!"

"Yes, that wanker. You two are fine ones to talk. You shouldn't have trashed his place like you did."

"Oh, really? And what way should we have trashed his dump? Anyway, we were only demonstrating the theory of the Big Bang to him. I thought he'd enjoy it."

"Yeah," Beyond interjected, "everything moves outwards. Like, all the time. Outwards. Yeah. Jodrell Bank ... hey, that's a good one, Jupe!"

"Listen!" Jane exclaimed. "I just came to tell you that Hocus-Pocus says if you go round and clear things up he'll let you back into class. Otherwise you're expelled."

It was Eddie's turn to spit. "I don't need school no more. I'm gonna be seeking out new lives and new civilisations and stuff, so old Hocus-Pocus can go hang." He turned to face Beyond. "You ready for another one yet, Be, or are you prepared to concede I'm the champ?"

"You're the champ, Jupe. Ah, Jodrell Bank, what a good one!"

"What about you, sis?" Eddie leered. "Can girls do all this sort of stuff?"

Jane turned away, walked back through the undergrowth, wondering what she'd tell Mother. Didn't the Bible say something about it was better to save a prodigal son than just any old Joe? She hoped it was true.

Jupiter took his closest friends
Out to Galactic Springs,
But, by Jove, he did not play fair
And grabbed the best of things.
Now Neptune's giving him
The old, cold shoulder
And Saturn hardly rings.

*

Like Kate Bush said, we're all grown up now. And moved away from childhood Edens.

Jane's little boy is at the childminder's. Her newish baby is asleep upstairs. And I'm back here alone with her after those years of separation and I look around her kitchen and see spick and span by the score and newly polished pine and lightness and airiness. The CD player emits Mozart. A copy of *Pour Elle* on the dining table bears the headline, "Masturbation – The Last Taboo?" It reminds me of a poster I had on my wall in college which read, "Wan King – Safe Sex Capital Of The World".

We are childhood friends. Teenage companions. She left for a career and a marriage to a man who has treated her well. In a material sense. But what exists between us cannot be denied for all eternity. We are adults now. Mature beings thrown back together first by chance and then by desire.

It's one visit. And then a return. Followed by a facile excuse to call round again. Repeated knockings at her portal with no real reason other than to be with her. She says she can't be unfaithful. She says she doesn't want to hold back with me any longer. She says we must be careful. She says she wants to lose control.

I am aching in my jeans pressed against her. Her fingers under my shirt are gentle moths devouring the fabric. Her small breasts are the first phases of the moon. Our clothes are an asteroid belt around our feet. She shows me how to make her come without any penetration. She is wildly thrashing, an umbilical cord come loose in the vacuum. My heart and my throat are almost weightless, my bare back Kelvin cold. I want the big explosion with her. I want the stars behind the eyes. I want her hands as creator, her lips mumbling let there be light … lust … love.

And there is love.

*

In my more spiritual moments I believe that we are but mummers in the pale re-enactment of God's creation. We are flickering shadows of no significance in any broader scheme. Every pulling of a curtain to separate our night and our day; every planting of a seed; every act of procreation and childbirth – they are all our vain yet unceasing attempts to mirror the original Creation.

The only pattern we can impose on the world is our own limited span of consciousness: If she comes back to me then there is a God and He loves Humankind.

All interpretations of the universe are inherently selfish.

All thought is mental masturbation.

The Last Martian Artefact

♂

There is something irredeemably macho about this blasted planet. To a greater or lesser extent, Mars is bringing out the ape in all of us. Simple things at first – Wild Jack recounting tales of shooting rabbits and racoons back home on his ranch, Eddie using our recreation time to set up an arm wrestling league... all the usual bad boy stuff. This morning, however, I had to intervene in a commotion between Philip and Dave which promised to end with pistols at dawn. My final card was to insist that we all needed to stick together for the present in order to face the far greater danger posed by the native inhabitants of this desert place. 'Krieg in sicht!' – the old rallying cry to unite against the common enemy.

But I'm uncertain as to how much I believe the perceived threat myself.

Michael looked again at the newspaper photographs. They should have been blue-green on red but they were black and white just like the photocopies he'd obtained from the library. These pictures had been taken by British astronomers based in Tenerife, using something called a Van Helsing filter. They showed a pattern of – what? Fault-lines? Fissures? Dried-up riverbeds? Doubtless the current manned expedition intended to answer the question fully; for the moment it was clear that Schiaparelli's Martian canals were more than a mere delusion.

He ought to be doing his Maths GCSE assignment, but... The sooner he could leave school, the better. They didn't appreciate the manner of his intellect. They thought he was just a failed nerd, a not very bright geek. Yet secretly he'd accomplished an intuitive leap and seen something no one else had -

"What are you doing?" his mother asked, entering the room without knocking.

"Oh, just some homework, Mum."

God, parents! What if he'd been having a Jodrell Bank?

"Well, your tea will be ready in five minutes. *Neighbours* is on if you want to watch it."

"No thanks, Mum. Busy."

"That's nice. Can I look?"

"Er, no, it's special research," he answered, covering the papers' aboriginal souls.

"Suit yourself, dear."

She exited.

Neighbours, late meals, intrusive parents – he would be shot of all that soon. He had some belongings already packed. If he could just rustle up some more cash from somewhere.

Allowing for an astonishing difference in scale, Michael had discovered that, by accident or design, the under-used and half-forgotten canals of inner London were modelled almost exactly on their Martian counterparts.

The manned mission was pretty close to reaching Mars. He hadn't been chosen for the crew; he hadn't even known until recently how this trek to the fourth planet was going to open up the previously hidden possibilities of his young life. No space trip ever succeeded without proper ground support and Michael had got over his delayed disappointment at not making the voyage. His role would be at least as important as Cooper, Wylie and the rest. As soon as Terrapin One landed, he would set up camp alongside Regents Park Canal. He intended to shadow their mission. That was the key to everything.

"Your tea's ready, Michael!'

That was the key to everything.

*

Surface close, Mars is actually more brown than red. We have seen no sign yet of the infamous canals. Mission Control promises to computer-guide us from Earth base along their apparent channels.

There was a war here many millions of years ago. The air is thin with carbon dioxide but thick with dormant ghosts. If we yet dared remove our facemasks, I'm sure the prevailing odour would be that of death.

They're back! the posters screamed.

Blood red on fluorescent blue. In slightly smaller letters: And this time they're immune to bacteria!

Days later, a new campaign with a further explication of the who: Now the Martians look just like us. Be careful who you trust.

A spoof – or was it? – news report on local cable showed a multiracial gang of vigilantes unmasking the dirty, transformed invader from the fourth planet. Couch potatoes were up in arms.

You too can help us Earthies spot these alien impostors from the planet of war. Look out for the following tell-tale signs: their skin is perfectly hairless and of an underlying red complexion. They are uniformly male. Our Earth mothers are beyond reproach but we might have to stand up and fight like men to keep it that way. An extended April Fool's jest? A media conspiracy? Or the free press exposing yet another government cover-up? Some people were willing to believe anything.

The story grew hyperbolically from a slow burn of isolated tales of lynch mobs, hapless victims and smashed-in store fronts as citizens armed and supplied themselves for a lengthy siege.

They're over-macho, over the moon and over here.

Post-Iraq / Afghanistan / Syria technology won't save us this time. We need a touch of Falklands bravado or, better still, the good old Blitz Spirit to see us through.

In the asteroid belt nothing quite fits together.

Unidentified bombers – Martian spies, freedom fighters, Middle East terrorists, who knew? – took out the Houses of Parliament. Guy Fawkes had died of shame some four hundred years earlier and was not present to see his life's mission finally completed. A handful of members were scattered into the murky grey Thames. Few tears were shed: these guys were zombies at best, aliens at worst.

Then came the final push towards anarchy – a rogue announcement on Radio Four:

"Fellow Britons, many would tell you that Japan, China, Germany, America and such like have superseded us on the world stage; but we know better. When the Martians last invaded in 1898 they began their assault in the Home Counties. It is obvious that they would begin in the South East again when they returned to take their bloody revenge.

"All Englishmen now abed; arise!

"Fe fi fo fum, let's go kill some Martian scum!"

For a final touch, a melodramatic:

"Aagh – "

A rattle of gunfire – or maybe it was knocked-over crockery. They were pretty hot with the convincing special effects, these technicians. Orson Welles had blazed the glorious path.

Sounds of a scuffle. Then a calm, reassuring voice:

"Here is the shipping forecast."

But no, Brian, we are no longer calm and we are not reassured. Let the bout begin and may the best man win.

She woke me with the almost-welcome words, "Gosh, you were wild last night!'

My throat was still raw from the sandstorms. I staggered up and out to my bathroom to both drink and relieve. A quick glance through my bedroom window assured me I was back in London and doubtless had been all night despite forceful impressions to the contrary. I had fallen asleep wearing just an old green T-shirt, my body pressed up against Jane's white buttocks. Then I was transformed into a being somewhat taller, broad-shouldered, maybe winged, rising up majestically to envelop my love…

There were very few females on Mars. Even this dream or projection may have been a long-distant memory. The pink sky would have held the romance of sunset if the planet were not so damn cold and dusty at this bleak season. We walked and then made love on a beach that had waited overlong for the never-returning tide.

"God, I hope I took precautions," I muttered over my earthly coffee.

"Fortunately, I did," she smiled.

"Are you okay?" I asked. "I mean, I wasn't too rough, was I? It's all a bit mixed up with a dream I was having."

"I'm okay." Her black hair was unruly and her white silk blouse had become creased. "What did you dream about, Simon?"

"Mars again. I was one of the original inhabitants, I suppose. I've got a feeling that I'm getting close to some sort of psychic revelation about them – though why this should happen to me I don't understand."

She was putting things into her overnight bag. "Gosh, is that the time? I've got to be going!"

"What will your husband say?"

"It's all right, I can take care of that."

"When can I see you again?"

"I don't know. We'll have to see."

"Jane, stay here. Let things come to a head."

"No, I must go now. Really." Then, as she left: "Be careful what you dream, Simon."

I have to report Joe's death. At Wild Jack's instigation, if not actual bloodstained hands. Also, nothing has been heard of David since his declaration that the atmosphere was perfectly breathable and we were 'a bunch of sissies' to bother with oxygen apparatus.

It seems clear to me that we have been possessed by the malevolent spirits who once inhabited but latterly destroyed their civilisation on this planet. Throughout our fractious sojourn I have sought to bury myself in detective work. What I have been able to piece together from surviving cave paintings and other archaeological records leads me to believe that the late Martians had dispensed with the female sex and were also gearing up for a full-scale invasion of the third planet. Only internecine strife stopped them. Their influence and evil intent lingers on, however, and the longer we remain here the more infected we Earth men become.

If we leave now me might yet save ourselves. But if we go home we might be carrying the murderous plague with us.

Everybody was becoming more and more suspicious of everyone else. At first it was mostly in fun, rather like the old seaside custom of challenging the man in the sunglasses and brown derby with: "You are Mr Bogeyman of the Daily Mirror and I claim my £10 reward." Soon, however, a capacity for mischief and thuggery was revealed. Back streets, pubs and rambling council estates resounded to the cries of:

"He's a Marshy, let's do 'im!"

In a desperate attempt to contain public order, television and newspapers released exact details of what to look out for, while maintaining that the whole thing was a piece of fiction to boost ratings and shift a whole pile of imported merchandise.

"A defining feature of the masquerading Martian is his lack of facial hair."

Teenage girls plastered their walls with pictures of bearded but still doe-eyed pop stars. Most men kept at least a healthy stubble on their chin, which was always ready for close inspection in case of forgery. "Oh, John, I wish you'd shave, your skin is tickling me" became "Mmm, yes, darling, I do like a man with a bit of rough."

It was noted that many Native American tribes lacked facial hair. It was also noted that they were, erroneously in most cases, thought of as having red skins. Red being the surface colour of Mars, it was a simple illogical step to tar them with the Martian brush. One creation myth spoke of the world being carried on the back of a giant turtle. The fact that the first manned flight to the fourth planet was on board the spaceship Terrapin One could be no coincidence.

Fortunately, there was not a noticeably large population of Native Americans living in paranoid Britain and those that were present kept a very low profile. The wiser people amongst the whiter-skinned avoided sun lamps for the time being, just in case.

My Encyclopaedia Computica assures me:
"There are no Martians. There never were."
I type in:
"Ideas never die."

I have been confined to quarters. Twice a day rations are brought to the door, once a day my captors replace my bladder sac. I suppose Philip, Wild Jack and the rest of my erstwhile colleagues think they're behaving in a civilised manner by keeping me alive. It's been rather too many million miles of weightless travel to enjoy ending up with a metaphorical ball and chain!

We have got the Martians wrong. I believe that instead of warring they were in fact experimenting with what these days we call 'terra-forming'. Deimos and Phobos, those orbiting gonads, were simply early failures. That their efforts eventually culminated in this pockmarked, sand blasted, atmosphere-free world does not detract from the grandeur of their scheme. My dreams are all of pyramids, Easter Island statues and the Manchester Ship Canal. So many untold influences on our consciousness...

I believe the rest of the crew has a grandiose plan to convert our nuclear powered craft into a massive bomb. They have the stink of martyrdom about them. Whether they intend to blow away the relics and the memories here or return to Earth and further disrupt the geosphere, I can only wait and conjecture.

British social order was going to hell in a handcart. Jerry dutifully continued to walk along the cratered streets to the office every morning but... to what purpose and for how much longer? The commonly accepted explanation was that the Mars mission had somehow unlocked a deadly time capsule and the Earth was acting as a giant receiver dish for the race memories of the long extinct Martians.

"Bastards," Jerry cursed, turning the corner into Bethnal Green Road. "Not content with destroying their own world, the poxy Martians are messing up ours, too!"

Of course, there were the usual apologists and bleeding hearts pleading clemency – be nice to the million year dead macho thugs, they didn't really mean to exterminate all their women, that was just a story, they were gentle and artistic people really...

"Piece of crap," he muttered, ignoring the red man on the pelican crossing.

"Hey, kid!" someone called from an alleyway.

"I'm not a kid, I'm twenty-two!" he yelled back and then regretted answering.

"All right, young man! Come and see what I've got." Jerry shook his head, began walking swiftly, but the stranger added, "You want to stop having bad dreams about the Martians, don't you?"

Cautiously, Jerry walked over to the doorway. The guy was holding some unremarkable rocks. He was the first man Jerry had seen for weeks who didn't have a beard or at least stubble.

"You know what these are?" the stranger asked. "No? You're familiar with the principle of Kryptonite, I take it?"

"Sure. Superman loses all his powers."

"These are Martian artefacts. Perfect protection."

Jerry sniffed. "Forget it, mate. I'm not buying some rubble you just picked up from a building site."

The shadowy vendor shook his head. "Please, my friend, take them for nothing. I want you to have them."

Jerry reluctantly complied. Maybe they had some talismanic power, maybe not. You couldn't be certain of anything these days.

When he reached his workstation the manager informed him that the electricity supply was off again and the office would be closed until further notice.

On the way home, despite his full light brown beard and milk-white skin, Jerry was chased by a bunch of young vigilantes. He eventually took shelter in a burned-out clothing factory. In the process, however, he mislaid the magic stones. Carefully retracing his last dozen steps, he picked up some likely looking bits of red rock but he couldn't be 100% certain they were protective Martian ore.

He would find out later, however...

Why bother with the huge investment of time and money – not to mention the unforeseen repercussions – of sending a manned flight to the outermost rocky planet? The Mount Everest answer – "Why climb it? Because it's there!" – will not suffice in this case. Only three theories safely squeeze through the airlock.

Maybe it's the old JFK and LBJ trick – the space programme as a distraction from increasing problems at home.

Or else, top secret advances in technology offer us the opportunity of fleeing this dying home world and terra-forming Mars into the root myth of 'a new Eden'. Each successive astronaut has gazed back and found our magic marble a little less blue. This is the fire drill. Know and remember your exit.

My last conjecture is a development of the second. The big red pebble might be an acceptable place to send all the 'difficult' citizens – Mars as a twenty-first century desert island or, indeed, Australian outback?

There's some frozen water up north and there's almost an atmosphere.

Here's some seeds and a shovel, boys, now get on with it!

*

Most people know that Romulus and Remus, founders of Rome, had a wolf stepmother. Less commonly known is that their father was Mars, or Ares, the god of war and agriculture. The Romans bestrode the globe for a few centuries before capitulating to a mixture of rugged barbarians, a mystery cult which would not go away and the Empire's own internal divisions.

Been and gone.

On the red planet the push towards a flowering – or should that read a muscling? – of masculinity proved unstoppable. Some would say the Martians were mere fighting machines waging ever bloodier war against each other. Some would claim they were poets of pugilism, artists of artillery and attrition.

Been and gone also. The planet's surface is cratered and pockmarked, a glorified dust bowl. The atmosphere has been bombed out into the ether. Mars is as radioactive as hell although our instruments aren't subtle enough yet to detect its skewed isotopes. Beware.

The last Martian artefact is the planet itself, hung lifeless in the void with its two pathetic, irregular moons.

It's a warning.

It's our future.

The Call of Uranus

☉

Astronomy books tell us that Uranus was discovered in 1781 by Sir William Herschel, a German-born British musician. In fact, the old man's planet did not exist at all before that date and was actually invented, but subsequently mislaid, by Herschel's great rival Haydn as a necessary element in an unusually dramatic baroque concerto. Careless translations of their correspondence have rendered the exact situation uncertain, with claimants supporting the ambitions of either side. Received wisdom claims Herschel discovered Uranus while searching for a comet, although my Schwarz Und Weiss version from 1815 substitutes the word 'crotchet'.

I remember making love with Sally while she was pregnant. In some cultures there's a taboo against such intercourse but to me it seemed a natural continuation of our physical love. I was twenty-something, moved up to London, looking for work, hope, a new love… whatever succour the great metropolis offered.

Sally had become uncomfortable lying on the bed, so I'd stood behind her, pressed against her smooth bottom, feeling the damp cotton of her rolled-up maternity dress against my bare chest. My arms looped around her, holding the warm burden of her belly like some exotic fruit. I wondered if the baby was aware of the gentle thrusts causing minor tremors through the humid womb. Sally's breasts were already producing tiny hard pearls in readiness for the hungry male mouth.

"Be careful, Simon," she said, "don't harm the precious gift."

"I couldn't bear to hurt him or you. But I want him to know me. I want him to know his origins... Everybody wants to know their origins, it's only natural..."

Sometimes when Sally was asleep, I'd carefully place my arms over her roundness and whisper to the growing baby. All the books and all the pre-parental classes were focused on the then current buzzword of 'bonding'.

I don't remember what I said then. I know the sort of things I'd say now:

"I want you to know who you are and where you come from. Even though the universe shifts away from us and I become just a monthly maintenance cheque... just a blurred photo and an absence maybe as vast as the void itself or as insignificant as the space between two electrons... even though I'm just another statistic in the modern male condition..."

Space, embryos, new generations of living creatures: it was just your normal, everyday miracle, that's all. The giant tree from the tiny seed; the glowering, world-destroying human from the microscopic conjunction of sperm and egg... the apparently infinite universe from one cataclysmic moment of concentration and creation.

Aquarius
Your ruling planet Uranus has moved into the ascendant sign on your chart causing possible disruptions and reversals. Be prepared to move heaven and earth in order to stand your ground.

*

I obtained employment working on a travel brochure. The pay was by commission only. The company was trying to set up something new for the adventurer jaded by white water bungee war zone safaris. Price was no object. I was asked to come up with something for the planet Uranus. Nobody had ever expressed an interest in going there. It was a one-horse town and in fact many of the local inhabitants were desperate to get off-world and head here.

I tried to sell the venue on the idea that it was the most unusual destination in the solar system, a planet turned so far on its side that summer and winter were each forty-two years long. Perhaps that was too much of a step up from the six-month seasons of the Arctic and the Antarctic.

The godforsaken hellhole didn't really possess the necessary Wastelands/ wild frontier frisson to put bums on seats and eventually I gave up in despair.

I resigned my post, three months older and a thousand pounds living expenses poorer. It's a shame. It was a good job while it lasted.

It is God's wish that every planet in the solar system either is, was, or will be inhabited. It is humanity's myopia to be unable to detect life forms which have no earthly parallel.

Uranus is covered with methane ice. CH_4. Frozen marsh gas. Many Uranians are therefore held in suspended animation but several of these vaporous creatures have cast their lightweight eyes over the blue and white planet with a view to evolving into beings suited to warmer climes. Their gaseous nature has enabled them to drift across the vast reaches of the ether and, for the moment, take up parasitic residence inside the more magically mysterious and cold blooded of our Earth-people: dentists... wheel clampers... loan arrangers. There are probably one or two of these possessed characters already in your circle of acquaintances.

*

It was a slow afternoon in the Department for Back Tracking Antiquities. Caroline, the line manager, was out at a conference, leaving Edison nominally in charge. All the ingredients were in place for another round of merciless ribbing of long-suffering Alfred.

"Hey, Tracey, you heard about trainspotters? Yeah, well, Uncle Albert's a more advanced life-form – he's a star spotter."

"I spotted some stars once, Paul."

"Where was that, then?"

"Down the West End, of course, at a film premiere!"

"I sometimes spot the stars as well. They're normally on page 23, just after the TV and satellite listings."

"Yeah, Sandra. I'm an Aries man myself."

"Ooh, nice. Sweet young Virgo seeks powerful ram for moonlight drives."

"Fiery Scorpio has got a sting in her tail."

"What about Old Uncle Albert? What star sign are you, Alfie?"

Softly: "Taurus. "

"You're talking bull, mate. Ha ha ha!"

On and on. Admittedly no one's life or death giro was in the balance but they'd have to clear the top of their in-trays some time. Couldn't they all just coexist in peace? But even as far back as Cain and Abel that hadn't proved possible.

Five-thirty at last. Time to slope off back to his unfurnished bedsit.

"So, Alfie, not joining us down the pub, then?"

Another interruption: "Nah, Edi, you know Old Uncle Albert, he's off to play with his telescope. It's going to get longer and then shorter again..."

*

Leo

Work is extremely well starred this month. People who have previously undervalued you now come to appreciate the true wealth of your leonine talents. This may be just the moment to ask for assistance – financial and otherwise – for that pet project you have held as a mental treasure for so long.

Mr Holkham was cross with his radio. There were so many pirates these days or garrulous foreigners babbling and playing outlandish ethnic music. Holkham blamed the Common Market or European Community or whatever Fancy Dan label they'd affixed this week. Since the death of his dear lady wife some two decades ago he'd found solace in the BBC's classical music schedules, taking the occasional interesting play as a spoken diversion. Nothing too modern, of course, none of those show-tunes or cuss-a-thons that passed for popular culture. How annoying, then, even on FM, even on an expensive assemble-it-yourself Japanese job that there was always audible interference. Over the years, he'd become used to the reception problems of being on the North Sea coast – heck, you couldn't even get Channel Five on terrestrial telly, not that you'd want it – but on this apparently digitally self-tuning radio he was still picking up shrieks and whoops rising and fading like the waves of the ocean... or irritating snatches of turgid accordions. But when you tried to actually tune in to the strains of Radio Free Magyar or whatever tinpot transmitter it was, the signal was no longer there. Did the beam act as some sort of parasite, hitching a lift on the back of Radio 3 because it had no independent life of its own? Or was it something more sinister? You couldn't blame the Russians any more because the Cold War was over. Apparently. Perhaps it was some antigovernment force, some bunch of longhaired travellers in a pantechnicon trying to undermine all that was good and decent in British society?

Or else, and this only occurred to him after watching a rather puzzling edition of *Horizon* on telly, maybe consumer technology had advanced so far that even a midi system like his was able to pick up the background noise of the stars, the entropic conversations criss-crossing the constellations. Were the strange voices and unearthly caterwauling even human in origin?

"Too fanciful!" Violet would have said. But she had always been a very down to earth sort.

Light, music, radiation – it was all one wave or another. Waking, sleeping – it was all one wave or another.

Uranus is ringed, like all but the puniest planets. This would seem to be something to do with a property of gravity which we don't fully understand as yet, but it has been suggested that the rings give the planet the right stability and balance in the vacuum of space and stop it spiralling off into the distant ether.

It was true: Alfred Peckham really had set up a little desk sign at his work station at the Department for Back Tracking Antiquities which read: 'We are all just dust mites in the greater scheme of things'. It was a direct quote from his masterwork.

Furthermore, he was a published author, of sorts. And not just his self-published pamphlets of wisdom and speculation available in the more esoteric second hand bookshops across the land from London's Crouch End to the coastal resorts of Sheringham and Shiplea. Those silly, young, lager drinking pups he shared the office with would be surprised, maybe even impressed, to learn that he also spent his spare time writing letters and short articles which he sent by first class post to various popular magazines of the sort that one could pick up at the tube station or supermarket.

Lately, however, the replies had all been along the lines of: "Dear Uncle Albert, we regret that our readers just aren't interested in the birth of the solar system or quasi-religious theories. Perhaps you would like to send us some more of your amusing weather anecdotes or, better still, your brilliant indoor gardening tips."

A two-column article in *The Times* had recently suggested that the bout of radio and telecommunications interference was due to unusual magnetic shifts emanating from the surface of Uranus. Mr Holkham always chuckled at the planet's unfortunate name. Back in the stricter school code of yesteryear, such puns had been gleefully grasped. "Here, Perkins, last night I saw your anus!" was guaranteed to pop the ink cartridges of mirth during the most tedious Latin declension. Later, the Americans came along and started calling the place 'Urine-us' which the slightly older Holkham perceived as more a faux pas than a piss-take.

Bottoms. Farts. Lavatory sounds and odours. When his lonely retirement seemed just so awful he liked to cling on to the memory of good solid belly laughs from the days of yore.

It was a very British way to behave.

Many people down the centuries have questioned why the planet Uranus is turned on its side. The only acceptable explanation is that this is an act of defiance and goes some way to explaining why such a large object took so long to come into plain sight.

*

They'd stopped setting up the practical jokes at work, but the attitude towards 'Uncle Albert' was still dismissive at best, antagonistic at worst.

"You don't make it any easier on yourself," his line manager, Caroline Thorpe, explained.

"How's that? I answer their questions to the best of my belief and knowledge. If I have hobbies they don't share, frankly it's none of their business."

Ms Thorpe pursed her lips, straightened the cuff of her immaculate white blouse. "Alfred," she began, "please understand I am not criticising your work. As a person I find you inoffensive, but other members of staff have found you overzealous in your views. I've got nothing against strong beliefs – religious, political, whatever – but it's not always appropriate to express them in the work-place."

So that was it: the typical pressure to be a carbon copy of everybody else. Speak no different, think no different, act no different. And all he'd done was illustrate Humankind's humility in the face of the universe. But what did these young whippersnappers know about humility? Conformity, yes; humility, push off!

"We are all dust mites," he'd declared. "Tiny little crawling things in a barely dimensional world. All we can see is the carpet, and that's almost flat. We think it stretches on forever, because we're too weak to ever reach the edge of the sitting room. What do we know of the walls and the windows, the other rooms in the house, the garden and the street, the town and the big wide world? But, and this is the conceit, no doubt the dust mite has got what he thinks are some all-inclusive theories."

"You keep your bugs to yourself, granddad!"

"Yeah, and watch what you do with that vacuum cleaner nozzle!"

"Ow, nasty! Still, probably wouldn't matter much to Uncle Albert, know what I mean?"

*

Sometimes Mr Holkham would bump into his ex-pupils during his nightly combing of Shiplea beach. Not all of them had left the town, contrary to scare stories in the local paper about an ageing, decaying indigenous population. He remembered a few names and faces but was loath to even pass the time of day with the unreformed scallywags. Wearing headphones and concentrating on the hypnotic pendulum swing of his metal detector, he could pretend that he didn't hear their raucous greeting of, "Look, there's Mr Hocus-Pocus; how're you doing, you old fish fry?"

And in truth he was listening hard to the sounds of the Earth's breast rising and falling, seeking the cancerous man-made objects which gave off a different frequency from within her tainted skin...

And when the moon and stars were up, he'd raise his technological wand and point it at the deepening sky in order to hear mighty Saturn calling out to mad Uranus; or the broken rocks of the asteroid belt pleading, "Let's get back together, let's give it another try..." and beyond them the far-off, sizzling egg in a pan remnant of the Big Bang itself. Echoing all the way from the original moment of creation back down to a lonely old man on a beach in East Anglia searching for pennies and wristwatches and a time unimaginably distant. At about 10pm, earlier if there was any sign of rain, he'd shuffle off home to his hot cocoa and his crackly recording of Sir William Herschel's third symphony... and another oasis of meaning in the protracted heat-death of the universe.

There had lately been much consternation at The William Herschel Institute for the Advancement of Music over apparent jamming activities by their concert and radio station rivals, The Clyde Tombaugh Minimalists. Most confusing of all, however, was that the leakage and competing signals were not simply satellite-relayed but appeared to originate off-Earth. Many wild theories were put forward by the mostly female staff of the Herschel Institute which the (male) director had tended to dismiss as mainly unscientific whimsy. Witness: The Martian canal system was equivalent to Earth's ley lines and caused magnetic interference which manifested itself in the form of ghostly voices and the hissing rasp of rockets and flame-throwers. Or: The dark, mysterious, tilted planet Uranus way off at the edge of the solar system was acting as an enormous mirror for the Tombaugh Minimalists' projection (but how did they get their timings so accurate?).

At least the girls were showing some imagination, the director reasoned, which was more than the usual clutch of secretaries and research assistants had ever exhibited previously. There was some real talent in their ranks, that was for certain. Like the monkeys on typewriters producing Shakespeare plays, soon enough somebody would hit on a universal truth. He resolved to give each suggestion a fairer hearing.

Given the girls' predilection for the fantastical, maybe the Institute should redirect its energies into fiction or invest heavily in that headset-reality business.

Then again, music must advance. The whole world was donning headphones or sporting tinny mobiles and moving to a constant download soundtrack of popular sounds. The earthly effects caused by the outer planets were undeniable to anyone in the know. This was the dawning of the age of astrology and Virtual Reality and, as director, he had to keep the William Herschel Institute at the cutting edge. Every idea was worth proper consideration. Ley lines, canals, mirrors, tilted orbits, the Big Bang echoing through the tiny speaker of a Samsung… never completely rule out any possibility.

Today's crackpots are tomorrow's visionaries.

Alfie was just settling down for an evening's easy listening to recent CD renderings of Sir William Herschel's first three symphonies when there came the discordant warble of the doorbell. The caller was an ordinary looking bloke with tattooed forearms revealed by the working man's uniform of blue denims and black T-shirt.

"Yes?" Alfie asked a little nervously.

"I'm from the Residents' Committee. Did you read our recent leaflet, mate?"

"No, I didn't. Junk mail goes straight into the wicker file."

"Wicker file? Oh, I get you... Anyway, what we're looking for is volunteers. Squad members, so to speak."

"Are you a religious organisation?"

"What, in this day and age? We keep Christmas and Easter, but that's about it."

Behind him, Alfie could hear the extended timpani section which characterised Herschel's Uranus Suite. He hoped he could finish with the man before they started blowing the horns. Should never have opened the door in the first place.

"Just exactly what do you want?" Alfie demanded.

"We're starting a Normality Patrol. You know, like the government initiative they had in *The Sun* the other day. We need helpers to rid the area of weirdos and the like."

"Isn't the whole idea somewhat racist?"

"Oh no, not at all. We're pleased to welcome our, er, West Indian and Asian friends as long as they see things our way. No, mate, we're not the National Front or nothing."

The violins were chasing the violas as the allegro raced towards its climax. Alfie calculated he had about one and a half minutes digital time to get back for the best bit. Normality Patrol! Whatever next? Seemed more like an excuse for your local burglar to case the joint.

"I'll take one of your leaflets... and I promise to read it this time," Alfie muttered.

"When can I call back?" the neighbour asked.

"Uh ... I'll let you know."

The man smiled. "You won't regret this, Mr Peckham. We're building a better Britain. One fit for our children and our grandparents."

Alfie found he couldn't read and concentrate on the music at the same time. There was something very appealing about ridding the district of beggars, longhairs, sodomites, drivers of cars with decibel-busting sound systems and blacked-out windows ... council tax defaulters... trainspotters... people who didn't own televisions...

those who only washed their hair once a week... the list was endless.

"I'd like to see you guys try it," Alfie smirked. Then he thought of the ceaseless ribbing he endured at work and how one or two of the reprobates wouldn't need much of an excuse to take things a stage further.

"Maybe I wouldn't like to see you guys try it," he added.

Ridding the district of... Astronomers (but not star gazing horoscope merchants)... the feckless unemployed... novelists... classical music buffs...

Taurus

Sometimes even the most stoical and bullish of Taureans succumbs to stress. Fear not, however: the recent realignment of the astrological heavens, which has otherwise remained unchanged since the Assyrians' day, has tilted fortune in your favour. You will be rich, enjoy good fortune and possess many women!

You had to cherry-pick your time to visit The Wastelands. Sometimes it was safer than others. Mostly I liked to explore the perimeter.

From either crest, the valley looked deep and inviting. There had lately been a major clean-up operation to eradicate the encrusted filth and pollution but still our parents spoke darkly of the unnamed dangers.

Eddie was touting a monochrome picture liberated from a girlie magazine. The shot was all shaved white legs and an out of focus backside. Eddie claimed it was some shop assistant from Chesilham. Furthermore, she'd agreed to meet him upwind of the thin brown river, with promises of further penetrations and incursions. Jack had come along ostensibly to keep score, or maybe pick up the leftovers.

"Well now, me old oysters," Eddie announced with typical mock grandeur, "we have known both the mountains of Venus and also the more down to earth pleasures. It is time to trespass boldly once again."

"She's just some floosie from up the coast," Jack reminded him.

"Yeah, she's hardly one of our gang," I added.

"All the better," he smirked. "Who needs a flock of ice maidens like my poxy sister, eh, Simon?"

I didn't answer him. It was unnecessary. He knew how I felt about Jane; although I probably should have replied just to uphold her honour.

She'd said to me, "It's okay, just don't stray in too far."

"I'll keep my escape route open," I'd joked.

"You know what I mean," she'd answered with just enough annoyance that the whole escapade was almost called off. "It's more than just a game of dare. I don't want either of us getting hurt."

We were reckless teenagers, or so we thought. Our parents forbade us to enter The Wastelands, but with our moderate school grades and distaste for stealing cars or tractors, how else were we expected to rebel against the ruling generation?

Alfie's Almanac: Wisdom, Horoscopes and Weather Reports

The Normality Patrol already exists in your world as a prospect if not yet a proven fact. Yesterday's soothsayer and / or prophet would be today's schizophrenic. We are heading towards a homogenous future and I don't like it. As the feminists would say: "Freedom is the right to say no."

You probably knew all this already. You probably completely disagree with me.

Good.

Everything is written in the stars.

But not quite in the way we imagine.

Authors should be invisible. Readers want made-up stories with realistic characters, not real people.

All boundaries are in a state of flux. The apparent universe is still expanding, but the acceptable solar system is being made to contract.

Of course I'm a know-it-all! Wouldn't you be if you were as clever as I?

There was a time before us and there will be a time after us. All other beliefs are mere speculation.

The so-called 'Gaia Theory' needs to be taken to its limit. The answer came to me at an unexpected moment. Maybe it was just a deeper than usual sexual experience. Maybe the primary linkage of man, woman and six-month foetus opened my eyes to a realm beyond the physicality of my head on her shoulder, my penis inside her and my groin pressed against her damp white buttocks.

Everything, and I do mean absolutely everything, is linked as part of one immense living system. But the catch is that the whole expanding universe of which we are such a minute part is itself merely the developing embryo inside the womb of a much larger cosmos. We have yet to reach the stage which could be equated with birth.

Who can guess what awaits us then?

Mercury Me

RM Quicksilver Cerebral Interface Model Zero Zero One is now in standby mode. Please supply an operating system.

Any size brain will do.

```
Confidential Memo
    Thank you for your recent study. The ruling
council is broadly in agreement with your conclusions.
The site you have identified for the next round of
Rexxon nuclear tests expertly fulfils the requirement
for a barren landscape of no scientific or environmental
significance and is, of course, far enough from major
population centres to ensure minimum opposition from
Earthpeace and other noisy agitators.
    Well done!
    How about a beer some time?
    Peyton Farquar-Jones, Colonel (retired)
```

The rain had eased off and it was okay now for Dennis to open his bedroom window without causing damp rivulets to seep into the already rotting wood of the sill. He turned the tiny brass coloured key in the lock. London smelled fresh at last. He switched off the overhead light. Its 100-watt bulb emitted an unpleasant odour of burnt dust.

He couldn't see much of the night sky from his low-rise eyrie. Simon at work was intending to sneak up to Hampstead Heath with a strong pair of binoculars to try to observe the mushroom clouds on Mercury. Dennis wondered if he should have gone with him but he suspected Simon was taking his girlfriend along, which made the midnight assignation doubly dangerous.

It was so hard to meet anyone these days.

To his left, the box factory was closed for the night with only low-level security lighting disturbing its nocturnal reverie. Ahead and to the right were the unkempt back gardens and rear views of the terraced housing of Stool Street and Link Road. Several of the conversions remained unoccupied. A few showed illuminated rectangles of civilisation, mostly obscured by old blankets or tatty curtains. It was hard to keep track of some of the comings and goings but at a nautical angle of thirty degrees he'd spotted a young woman behind the window of her bedsit three nights ago and had maintained a regular vigil since. With luck she might be a student or a nurse or a social worker – someone at least with a little of the flame of liberalism undimmed within her heart.

It was so difficult to meet women these days.

He let the dark gather round him. The showers had abated but the sky was still overcast and starless which meant no nuclear test sightings of ill-treated Mercury tonight. Wasn't the innermost planet usually too close to the sun anyway to be studied in proper detail…?

In an unexpected twinkling, she was there: fully dressed, fair hair loose about her shoulders, white face and hands only partially in shadow. God, she was beautiful! Even from this distance, even with this lack of clarity.

She might not be able to see him unless he switched his bedroom light on again. He so wanted to reveal himself to her but was fearful of shocking with suddenness.

Her eyes – an indeterminate colour from so many yards away – turned and looked in his direction. It appeared that she'd seen him; his opening gambit had been successful. As he watched, she pressed her body against the pane, flattening her cotton-covered breasts provocatively against the glass. She seemed to be mouthing words, her lips and jaw making wild open kisses like an air-breathing mermaid as she soundlessly whispered, "Mercury me? ... Marry me...?"

Perhaps she understood Morse. It was important that he communicate with her. He scrabbled around for his pocket torch. The batteries were dead. There were half-alive nought percent cadmium ones in his razor in the bathroom. He was in such a rush that he initially put them in the wrong way round. They would have worked... in an antimatter universe.

By the time he was back in position, the young woman had thrown a Laura Ashley wrap over a rail above her window. Doubtless she had tired of waiting. He hoped he would see more of her tomorrow. It wasn't easy meeting available women these days.

I was researching various items of popular music from the later twentieth century and early noughties. Several major entertainment corporations had expressed a cursory interest in my work but would not front up any money until I had a more clearly defined product to offer them. To achieve this 'defined product' I needed money up front... and so on.

My latest scheme was to compile a rock 'n' roll response to Gustav Holst's The Planets. Instead of six or seven minutes for each, I envisaged a whole CD devoted to every planet in the solar system. I also entertained the notion of enlisting a computer wizard or film buff as a partner in order to produce suitable graphic or DVD accompaniment. The 1970s combo Manfred Mann's Earth Band had registered a chart hit with Joybringer, their take on Holst's Jupiter, the Bringer of Jollity but I wanted to go the whole hog.

Earth and Venus were relatively easy. I had a whole heap of Eve of Destruction / Blowing in the Wind / Protect Mother Earth type material for the former; love songs aplenty referencing the goddess for the latter.

For the body closest to the Sun, however, I was so far stuck with an out of date phone company jingle, a record company logo, Steve

Miller's Mercury Blues – about a car, for goodness sake! – and maybe one cut each from the cult bands Mercury Rev and The Quicksilver Messenger Service. Given the paucity of material, I was ready to make a case for the inclusion of Led Zeppelin's Communication Breakdown, which at least referred to the mythological aspects of the sphere's nomenclature.

Meanwhile I had to earn a pretty penny in order to eat. A failed pop singer and over-stiff actor, I had long been complimented on the texture and tone of my relaxed masculine speaking voice. A curious side effect of the government's various recent morality acts had been the sudden upsurge in companies offering telephone sex. Lacking the blue sash of the newly-wed, and indeed unable to persuade my then girlfriend to flout the new legislation and come to bed with me regardless, I had become something of a consumer of these salacious services myself for a few sorry months. The realisation eventually hit me that maybe there were also lonely or unfulfilled women seeking this aural solace. As get-rich-quick schemes go, this was pretty sure-fire. If she sees me across a crowded room she's hardly going to wet her knickers in anticipation, let's face it; but with her eyes closed or tucked up under the duvet, my vocal cords might yet help transport her to nirvana and beyond...

I invested heavily in newspaper advertising, under suitably Mediterranean sounding names. I sat back and waited. The calls came in.

They were all from rather tough sounding gay men.

Anybody know an Arts Foundation looking to fund a space music research project?

Progress Report
It is said that the majority of people on Earth are no longer employed in the hunter/gatherer/farmer occupations of our forefathers but instead are engaged in the dissemination of endless items of information. The world is abuzz with glorified gossip. Before too long a new range of cheap computers will affix directly onto

the cerebral synapses and enable the roadside cafes of the super-highway to witness a meeting of minds... or a melding into one unified, uniform view.

Up here on the planet Mercury the significant information from the solar system's super-highway is all about the planet's graveyard diurnal rotation and the expedition's constant repositioning, which movement enables us to stay within the slither of twilight where the surface temperature is just about bearable for human beings. It's all part of the daily chore.

We arrived back in the late 1950s. Our bulky, padded suits and fishbowl helmets have by now achieved a certain fashion presence. At least they're still working, as are the mobile hydroponics tanks. Genetically altered algae replenish the oxygen supplies. Our daily diet is a monotonous round of bio-engineered, high-protein rice, citrus and avocado derivatives. Fifty years of vegetarianism is enough for anybody! We receive yearly updates from Hollywood Base back on Earth but the planned relief mission has been cancelled so many times that nobody believes in it any more.

Mercury's lower gravity and proximity to old Sol seem to have slowed down the ageing process so that I count myself as yet being in the prime of life. Our mission commander has posed the following question: Does time itself run differently depending how close one is to the Sun? The variations on Earth would be negligible but here we seem to be noticing and benefiting from its effects. But as all human experience is essentially subjective, we can only conjecture…

Despite the fiery fountain of youth licking at the edges of the habitable zone, I fear that parts of me, however, may atrophy through disuse. Is sex still the major recreational sport back on Earth? Has it been replaced by pill popping; or else some method of plugging straight into the brain's orgasm centre?

We've been here a hell of a long time with our straight-backed all male crew. There is no local totty to speak of. It's so hard to meet pleasant, available women these days.

*

Sirs,

Further to your correspondent's enquiry regarding what is the correct political response to the government's prolonged nuclear testing programme on the planet Mercury, may I suggest that a unified boycott is in order?

Were we dealing with a foreign power it would be simple enough to stop purchasing their apples / wine / plastic toys / holiday offers and so forth. Given that it is our illustrious leaders who have landed us in this radioactive pickle, and as there is no sign of an election on the horizon for several years yet, we should seek to withhold both direct and indirect taxation.

For those whose PAYE is deducted at source the simple expedient of offering shops only the cost price of a range of goods – i.e. without the VAT – should suffice. If the store kicks up a fuss, write an IOU. After all, VAT is merely money that traders handle as a collecting point for the government and does not materially contribute to offsetting their running costs or add to their eventual profit; quite the opposite, in fact.

Yours,
Name and address supplied.

The British Normality Patrol Needs You!

Do you get stressed out by constantly having to endure graffiti, vandalism and noisy neighbours?

Do you want a better standard of living not just for your children but for yourself, too, before it gets too late?

Are you willing to spare two hours a week of your leisure time to make this country great again?

If you have answered YES to any or all of these questions, or if you simply share our concerns, we need you to get in touch with us as soon as possible. It's a big job ahead and we will only succeed through the strenuous efforts of committed volunteers.

Think about it:

No more hoodlums.

No more beatniks.

No more dissent.

The British Normality Patrol – We're on every corner!

The justification for our mission to the innermost planet is not simply 'Because it's there!' but for reasons relating to rocky planets in general. The Jane Wylie Theory of Planetary Evolution postulates that the four non-gaseous worlds will each in turn develop viable carbon-based life forms. Mars is history and if we're not extraordinarily careful for at least a further millennium, Earth will suffer a similar fate. Top secret reports suggest that Venus may soon be about ready to reach the Garden of Eden stage, which leaves boring old barren Mercury.

Such utopian ideas were commonplace in the novels and films I devoured during my misspent youth. Every theory has its day of scientific respectability, I suppose. Mercury's proximity to the Sun and its lack of atmosphere make sustainable life even less likely here than on the Moon. Also, this slowly turning ball of dust lacks the romantic associations we still hold for silvery shining Luna.

The captain has suggested that the multi-million mile journey and the huge conflagration of the yellow star burning mightily above our heads has in some way distorted our time sense. We believe our exploration is into its fifth decade when in fact the duration may be more correctly measured in months and weeks. Quite what the implications of such findings may be for future star-bound missions only time will tell.

My Darling Jolene,

I've thought long and hard about this. Given the current political climate, I understand your reluctance to 'go all the way'. As you have said, there is always the possibility that we will be 'found out'. Marriage has not been uppermost in my mind, but... there is no one else I would want to spend the rest of my days with and we're both grown adults, so...

Please don't think I'm simply proposing in order to have sex with you. As I've indicated before, I am not totally without experience between the bed covers but I have also learned to wait when occasion demands it.

These are difficult times for young or liberal thinking people. Together we will be much stronger.

With love as always,

Darren

Dennis had spent much of his free day wandering up and down Stool Street. His rudimentary geography placed the nocturnal woman on the first floor of number seventy-one. There was a 'Flat For Sale' notice just inside the front garden but he believed that referred to the damp and dingy basement. Every third building in the street harboured estate agents' grand proclamations but no one was buying.

Apart from one necessary return to his bathroom at shortly after three o'clock, Dennis passed the best part of six hours observing the comings and goings at number seventy-one. Except there were no comings and goings at all. Maybe she was out working all day on

Sundays. Perhaps she was a nurse or similar shift worker. He hoped she hadn't departed for a long holiday or been evicted or hurt in a traffic accident or mugged at Crosswire Station...

The dark satanic office blocks and tenements welcomed in their grey cloud cousins. After a light evening meal, Dennis once again stood sentry by his window, waiting for the vision who would call out to him... summon his aid, his arms, his amour...

There she was, at the window, wearing only a thin white shift of Gothic design but post-modern brevity. With the light behind her, he couldn't make out details of nipples and pubic hair, yet they were there, oh God, they were most certainly there... His window sill was just the wrong height, half shielding and hindering him as he pondered whether to reveal his fullness to her or take the voyeuristic pleasure alone by stepping backwards slightly. He felt like he was going to burst, a spray of hot white meteorites aching to hit the wood and the glass in a shower of stunted life...

He saw her lean backwards slightly, pull the nightdress over her flaxen hair, shake the tresses loose, which was exciting enough, then half turn and casually allow a 100-watt overhead bulb to illuminate the whiteness of her skin and the womanliness of her features... and Dennis could hold back no longer.

Again she had her face pressed right up against the window and seemed to be mouthing 'M' words: "Marry me...? Mercury me...? Manhandle me...?"

His security key for the lock on the handle was somewhere in one of the pockets of his discarded shell suit. When he'd wiped away a little of the ejaculatory mess, he would open his window and this time call out to the desperate, unfulfilled woman, assure her he would come and call, just as soon as his knees stopped trembling, because now there could be no turning back, they were united in love and lust forever...

She looked over her shoulder. Had some intruder entered her room? Dennis peered intently across the darkened gardens towards the oasis of light... and could just make out a naked man behind the window woman. Penis erect, the intruder in Dennis's dream let the woman fondle him for a few seconds then turned her so that he was once more entering from behind. Her moans were inaudible but the vibration of their shared orgasm rippled through the heat-blown silica, travelled casually and without hindrance through the cool night air above the yards and lawns, then burst with megaton force in the tackily detumescent bachelor pad of one who had watched... and lost.

"They came out of the side streets and hidey holes in their tatters or their Right-on designer label T-shirts and chinos, these rebels with a misguided cause, these indigenous refusniks. They carried banners and placards. Some carried weapons or whatever debris they could lay their hands on during their pedestrian journey. They screamed and bawled anti-government slogans littered with careless obscenities. Some called it a rising up of the community, others saw it for what it was: a last tail-wag of the dog-ends of society.

"Our police were ready for them, of course, and despite the occasional necessary tactical retreat, proved more than a match for this rag-bag of disorderlies and hooligan protesters. What began as a peaceful if rather pointless series of tax boycotts and other forms of non-violent but still illegal protests has inevitably led to this latest confrontation between the duly elected democratic forces of order and those who would scream their point of view from the blazing barricade and the trashed city. Be sure: our forefathers fought to make this island clean, independent and free and we will fight to eradicate once and for all the insurrectionist scum that lurks within the bowels of society and acts like a cancer at the very heart of post-modern Britain. Four letter words and petrol bombs may do us momentary harm but Right will triumph eventually.

"This is Gavin Meddler, BBC News, Central London."

Thetis wanted a strong son so she gave him the well-hard name of Achilles and bathed him in the River Styx, holding him under for so long that he nearly drowned. Only her hand and his heel were not submerged in the deep, deathly waters. This omission was to prove a fatal flaw in later life. Much better to have bought the warrior a pair of winged sandals like those sported by his cousin Mercury, messenger of the gods and patron of travellers and communications. Better still to tame Pegasus the winged horse, checking first to make sure the beast did not have Trojan parentage.

Back down here in the smog-clouded foothills and shanty towns far below ozone-rich Olympus, it's hard to tell what is fresh acid rain and what merely wax from the melting wings of Icarus. We kid ourselves that we are fleet of foot when, as latter-day philosopher-scientists are quick to point out, our walking motion is in fact a fall forwards, arrested, righted, continued over and over for the whole 26 miles and 385 yards... dreaming with every laboured breath of Shanks' winged pony...

Mercury was well up on all the godly gossip, speaking always of one greater who might yet phone home. Carried by his leather and feather shoes to the summit of Babel Tower, he surveyed the argumentative throng from this lofty eyrie and decided to create a new world language, which would in no way resemble Esperanto or any other grapho-phoneme system based on human speech or thought patterns. We'd all come a long way since wall paintings, drum beats, smoke signals, knots on ropes and Petrarchan sonnets. The global village needed something new yet elemental. This may once have been the language of Keats and Shakespeare, yet all linguistic refinements could easily be expressed by an extra chain of ones and zeros. Indeed, it was soon hard to remember why other systems had ever been thought either useful or necessary.

Everything and everyone could be reduced to a series of ones and zeros.

Zero One.

Zero One.

Zero zero zero.

0000000...

GIRLS, are you searching for the right man on whom to bestow your blue sash?

Then look no further!

QUICKSILVER INTRODUCTION AGENCY has hundreds of fanciable, solvent men on its books just waiting to splash the cash and pick up the tab.

Trained chaperones all part of the service.

Freephone 00000800 now.

Government Dating Licence: MER 121

Quicksilver Introductions – they're safer than inviting him in for coffee!

A slow but steady stream of pedestrians filtered past Dennis as he stood sentinel outside 71 Stool Street. There were the self-satisfied marrieds with their bright blue sashes; sullen singles of either sex taking unwarranted interest in paving stone features; and accompanied children, thankfully less voluble than of recent years. People, it seemed, were mostly adhering to the recent behavioural legislation. The 'For Sale' notice was still in place. Dennis knocked, waited...

"Yes, mate?"

"Uh, the agency sent me, uh," – a quick glance at the board – "er, Brian and Thetis."

"You'd better come in. Sorry about the stuff everywhere – I work from home, import and export and all that, you know..."

A coffee machine coughed raucously in the kitchen and a computer screen glowed greyly in the downstairs living room. There were cartons and half-opened crates everywhere. Within a minute

Dennis decided that the landlord – John something – was the thinnest wide boy he'd ever met.

There was a steep case of stairs partly concealed within a recess.

"Why are we going upstairs?" Dennis asked.

"It's where the flat is, mate. Didn't they tell you back at the office?"

"Oh, right. Just that I've already looked at a few places today. Getting confused"

As John opened a double-locked white wooden door, Dennis realised this was the room he'd partially observed from his own flat. But where was the orgasmic woman... and her frolicking fellow? He surreptitiously fingered the wallpaper, as if hoping to conjure up her spirit from the spilled pheromones.

"Didn't a married couple used to rent this place?" Dennis asked casually.

"That's right; though between you and me they might not have actually been legally wedded."

"What happened to them?"

"How should I know, pal? Maybe they ran off to Gretna Green or got abducted by aliens. Probably they were called up to do a foreign duty for the British Normality Patrol. What do I care? That was months back."

But he'd seen their fornication mere days ago. Was the man mistaken? Or lying for some obscure reason? Perhaps Dennis's own desperation and need had called their almost-ancient ghosts out of the yellow wallpaper into temporarily clear view.

While the landlord scratched his stubble, Dennis made a display of checking the plasterwork and fittings on the far wall whilst he took a long look across the back gardens towards his own window. This was definitely the site of the sexual act he'd furtively observed. He'd not expected to visit the place so easily... and with such disappointing results.

There was an apparent movement behind the net curtains of his own vacated bedroom. An intruder? An illusion? Or another necromantic conjuring act to defy the new British normality?

"You making an offer, then, mate?"

Shaking his head out of his reverie, Dennis declined.

"Never mind, someone will take it sooner or later," John consoled himself.

Dennis took one last lingering look around for memories and mementoes then followed the man downstairs.

"Here," said John, "you look a trustworthy sort. Local, aren't you?"

"Yeah."

"Got a girlfriend?"

"No."

"Well, if you do... and you want to make it official, like, I've got a whole stack of blue sashes I can lay my hands on. Genuine stuff, metal strip and everything. Dirt cheap. I've even got purple for the oldies. Give me a bell if there's anything you want to get hold of."

I could tell you, friend, Dennis thought, but I don't think she's the sort of commodity you're dealing in. She's lost. Forever.

The captain brings reports of strange tremors and flashes emanating from the night side of the planet. One of my colleagues compares the blast to that which obliterated Hiroshima and Nagasaki in my long-ago childhood. Is somebody testing A-bombs here? Have they not taken us into account? But did they take those thousands of Japanese civilians into account back in 1945?

We have passed several hours discussing the implications of an atomic explosion on a rocky world with no atmosphere to retain and rain down radiation poisoning. The captain advises caution. For my own part, I maintain a surface calm but underneath I am totally panic-stricken. We move camp every single day to avoid being either burnt or frozen. Our nomadic lifestyle means that inevitably we must soon cross the apparent blast zone. Five decades of successful off-Earth exploration wiped out in a -

Addendum to Previous Memo
From: Colonel Peyton Farquar-Jones (reinstated)
Classification: Top Secret
Gentlemen,
Sensationalist reports of a manned mission already present on Mercury and situated either partially or temporarily within the target zone have proved unfounded after thorough checks. (If they were there, they sure as hell ain't there now, folks!) We remain 100% certain that nobody's ever sent anybody – even in anger – to that hot and cold ball of rock. Rest assured, it's just another populist myth of the New Space Age.

Meanwhile, preliminary analysis of the missile test results on the surface has proved very illuminating as regards future pan-global strategy. We have come a long way since Robert Oppenheimer and the Manhattan Project. Now the challenge is to see what effect our weapons would have if we did what everyone has always wanted to do.

Which is: to build a whopping great weapon and target it directly at the original nuclear bomb...

The Sun.

First World Tour

You're not sure, but you've got an inkling that you're on your last legs. So, Gustav Holst is imagined to have taken his orchestra out on the road, playing his greatest hits to audiences both appreciative and with their own skewed agenda. If all this were true, I expect I would claim to have picked up his diary on Ebay. So, I have quoted liberally from this apocryphal document. – Allen

1933

Things are going from bad to worse. We have yet to receive any of the performance fees owed us from the week of concerts in Paris and the stopover in Seville. Audiences have been generally receptive to the old, familiar material but my new experimental piece The Asteroids – A Suite for Atonal Percussion was booed off the stage last night. I had to hastily arrange a quick segue into the Joybringer section from Jupiter to pacify the baying masses.

Crowd unrest I can cope with; disputes with star performers and purse-holding promoters are more problematic. We are down to a basic core of six players, picking up scratch musicians from the local dole queues barely hours ahead of each gig. I would say at least we've still got our first violinist Abraham Rosenberg but the local politicos here in Bremen have raised doubts about his fitness to play in front of the pure Aryan race. No one else can hold things together like dear old Abe and I am loath to bow to such demands, but there remain the veiled and not so veiled threats against both his person and mine if the concert goes ahead exactly as planned. The bullet hand-delivered to the hotel reception desk may not have been sterling silver but it certainly had my name upon it.

Such considerations have unfortunately forced me to delay introducing my new prodigy to the musically informed public. At twenty-one, James Marshall plays the trumpet with more aplomb than the Angel Gabriel. There is nothing I can teach him. My role is just to put the squiggles onto the barred paper then leave him to magic them into the beat of the body, the calm of the philosophical mind and the soundtrack of the heavenly afterlife. But these are not the speak-easies and jazz dens of New Orleans. If a Jew evokes angry protestations, what effect would a Negro have? Thus I have to hold him back for the moment – at the very most sit him in the shadowy wings covering the deficiencies of the saw scrapers and brass busters who pass for professional musicians in this dangerous continent. When the customs officers question us about his presence we say he polishes the instruments. Such talent! It's taken him out of the ghetto... to the position of a glorified shoeshine boy attached to a crotchety circus!

I'm getting too old for this touring lark. I almost wish I'd never written anything beyond the idle ostinatos of my student days. Fame is such a burden.

- Gustav

Sirs,

What is it that makes us so reductive with our heroes? So Gustav might have been a bit of a snob and somewhat reclusive once he'd made his dosh but, really, when you're talking popular music there's Robert Johnson, early Elvis and Holst's masterpiece The Planets. Everything else is just derivative.

Dead men can't answer back. Did Richard III really kill the princes in the Tower or was it just something Shakespeare made up to satisfy his royal benefactors? Likewise all these scandalous rumours concerning the great composer. Holst — a womaniser? Holst — a drug-taker? Holst a musical thief? Do me a favour! Why can't we just accept someone's brilliance without always trying to poke holes in justly earned reputations? The man made great music. In one hundred years' time people will still be humming his tunes. His revisionist biographers, on the other hand, will have moulted back into the slime from which they came.

I remain yours faithfully,
Colonel Peyton Farquar–Jones

Mistakenly, I'd thought that by setting out on a gruelling world tour I'd avoid the continual queries from the newsmen about both my professional and my private life. I'd put on my tuxedo and take up the baton for ninety minutes a night allowing the music to speak for itself.

Nothing speaks only for itself.

The piranhas attend the event but they choose to lounge in the bar while I'm conjuring magic from the five violinists. These fish-men come suddenly to air-breathing life after the gig and want to know what is the true nature of my relationship with Vaughan Williams.

"We're just good friends, for God's sake! Fellow musicians. I'm Gustav Holst, not Oscar Wilde!"

Then they're asking what is my response to the recent extension of the known solar system. Am I going to write a piece for Pluto?

"Well, gentlemen, I take a keen interest in astronomy, just as any other informed or educated person would, and all I can say is well done Clyde Tombaugh and the chaps. But my music is not about scientific reality. I'm a fabulist, a maker of myths."

Besides which, Pluto is associated with death and that's something I don't want to think too much about at present.

- Gustav

*

A Gustav Holst Chronology

c. 2000 BC – 30 BC: The time of the Ancient Greek, Cretan and Hellenistic civilisation.

753 BC: Romulus forsakes his wolf mother and founds the city of Rome on seven hills.

410 AD: Destruction of Rome by visiting Visigoths.

1543 AD: Polish astronomer Nikolai Copernicus suggests that the Earth and all other known planets orbit the sun.

1874: Gustav Holst, of Swedish descent, born in Cheltenham, England.

1892: Holst forsakes the commuter life and becomes a church organist.

1913: Holst begins work on Mars – The Bringer of War.

1919: First public performance of his magnum opus The Planets.

1934: Holst dies in London, England.

1958: Sweden hosts the football World Cup.

c. 1961: Art-house film director Ingmar Bergman (allegedly) lambasts the late composer for not being Swedishly sombre enough.

1968: Stanley Kubrick's monumental film 2001: A Space Odyssey is released. Holst's music does not feature on the soundtrack.

1970s/1980s/1990s: Cassettes replace vinyl and are then superseded by compact discs.

2000s and onwards: We're all listening on MP3 players, I-pads and tinny mobile phones in inappropriate public spaces.

1991: England hosts the Rugby World Cup and uses part of Holst's Jupiter as its theme music. The world appears to be in union.

c. 2020 AD to 2030 AD: The Olympian gods return to enslave Humankind and reclaim the Earth as their cosmic playground.

I've been offered the chance to break the mould of concert going.

"To drag classical music scraping and screeching into the twentieth century," as Mr Filmore puts it.

Simply, to relaunch The Planets as a sound and vision spectacular combining all available legal and hush-hush technology, creating an experience way beyond the dreams of grand opera. And, get this, we'll be using broadcast microphones for every instrument (aagh, hear every bum note in all its glory!) and playing sports stadia. Forget the Carnegie and the Albert Hall, suddenly I'm to take my music to the masses... and perform in venues more suited to burly plebeians booting a bag of leather up in the air than the delicate aesthetics of Venus or Neptune! It all sounds very fine in theory but the start-up costs are enormous and the break-even audience figure must be nearly ten thousand. Millions glued to the wireless is one thing, dragging hundreds of overcoated citizens into damp, cold terracing to listen in inclement weather to a piece easily available on a gramophone record ... well! I'm not sure society is ready for such cultural events just yet. The money is tempting – if I ever get to see any of it – but I'm a tad too cautious to be a symphonic Barnum. The whole project would doubtless collapse in utter ruin and my already wounded reputation would be in tatters.

- Gustav

*

A childhood asthmatic, son of a strict piano-playing father, short and bespectacled, his right hand often too weak to hold a fountain pen, Gustav Holst does not present as a sex, drugs and rock 'n' roller. While rehearsing Jupiter, a commotion from the cleaning women outside the hall disturbs him. They are dancing to his song of jollity!

"Ladies, sweet ladies!" he pleads. "This is a serious composition, not the music hall!"

In the days before Xerox and Microsoft, German prisoners of war are entrusted with the orchestral transcription. They mutter darkly amongst themselves, "Who is this Gustav menschen, eh? Is he secretly on our side or should he really be called Jeremy, Cuthbert or Quentin?"

Years later, Holst writes to his friend Ralph Vaughan Williams bemoaning the fame and media interest aroused by The Planets, which he now slightly dismissively refers to as Opus 32.

Vaughan Williams replies, "You should count your lucky stars, old son. After I die I'll be remembered solely for two tunes I borrowed from the court of King Henry!"

*

The neuritis in my arm is playing up again. Every time I lift the limb to indicate an upbeat I get at least a twinge; sometimes the pain is much, much greater. When I fell off the stage at Reading nearly ten years ago I vowed to take things easy in future but here I am again conducting a coterie of handpicked soloists and assorted hangers-on all the way round Europe for a pittance.

We play the same set every night and yet every night's performance is different. It is this intangible magic which still stirs my ageing blood. An irrational part of me believes that one evening we are going to achieve some sort of mystic apotheosis, playing, yea even creating, a perfect version which will open mystic doorways into...

into what, exactly? I studied much in my younger days, particularly mythology and the teachings of the ancient philosophers. Surely one of them must have had more than a mere inkling of the truth? But which?

Audiences are sometimes more informed than is generally supposed. It's the press who are morons! In my early thirties, I learned Sanskrit: the necromancer's tongue if ever there was one. As a consequence, I am occasionally approached after concerts by shy peasants or anonymous locals who wish to relate to me various superstitions, creation myths and tales told by their grandmothers. By the time I manage to write down the outlines I sometimes forget important details and have no way of cross-referencing the information. Doubtless, it all feeds into my work on some level but I often wish I possessed the more racy imagination of people such as Scott Fitzgerald or T.S. Eliot so as to make the best use of such a treasure-trove of human experience and wish fulfilment.

- Gustav

*

My first idea was to temporarily displace Gustav Holst and have him produce his finest work in the early 1960s, with The Planets setting the classical world alight contemporaneously with popular music's Beatlemania. Artistically, Holst then dries. However, The Beatles, Bob Dylan, The Doors, Jimi Hendrix et al cite him as a major influence and his work is never out of favour. As Psychedelia hits, questions begin to be asked about the great man's influences and artistic inspiration: specifically, did he turn on and tune in before San Francisco heads made LSD briefly fashionable? French Impressionism is now thought to have been partly fuelled by absinthe and marijuana. The lazy critical conceit is adopted by several leading rock commentators that for Holst to get such spaced out musical ideas he must have been, er, spaced out, man.

The Moon landings offer a promise which is never likely to be delivered, certainly not in our lifetime. Maybe the only solar system we can explore is as a concept and collection of myths, ideas and images of Venus, Mars, the Moon, etc.; to wit, the planets in our heads. Mind expanding drugs might help the creatively inclined undertake such a journey. Or else, there are other realms not accessible through mundane methods. Hallucinogenics, fasting, strict religious rituals, key sounds and visual signals... all of these may propel us towards a different reality.

Then again, perhaps what we see is all we'll ever have. Chemicals, cognac and classical music are just short-lived burns of escapism.

In this scenario, Holst becomes the one-hit wonder who squanders his royalties and whose critical standing plunges in tune with his expanding waistline and in inverse proportion to his intake of Class A stimulants. He crawls through the Slough of Despond, endures a messy divorce and several screaming tabloid revelations regarding his private life. More importantly, he believes he's lost everything... until he is suddenly rescued from acid casualty obscurity by a new breed of reverential young guitar players who champion his early work and bring it to the attention of a modem audience. His star rises again in the west. Record companies fall over themselves to reissue and repackage. A follow-up LP/CD is mooted. He publishes a ghost-written autobiography and does the round of chat shows extolling the virtues of clean-living after a life of excess, the easy moral of which is: "Have your fun young and pretend you're sorry now."

The new disc proves to be an utter disaster. Even guest appearances by Van Morrison, Diana Ross, Eminem and Pavarotti can't save it. Never mind, people simply go back to their CD re-mastering of The Planets to remind themselves of what all the fuss was about in the first place.

Gustav Holst dies quietly in a Malibu health clinic of an AIDS-related illness. The obituaries are all accompanied by a photo of the composer in his pomp.

*

Tonight's concert has been cancelled owing to equipment problems. Specifically, a lack of the right gauge strings for our cellist and violinists. Last night's show was one of the few unmitigated successes of this endless tour and I would have liked to build from such an achievement. Really, to be unable to obtain proper spares in supposedly civilised Europe is beyond belief. I have my suspicions that the local political bigwigs have somehow engineered the situation so that I am obliged to take up their offer of a three course dinner for myself and the principal members of the orchestra at the Zeitgeist Hotel. In the absence of my dear wife, I shall be accompanied by our lead soprano, Jane Weill. I am an old man and have been away from home rather too long. She offers me pleasant, even suppliant, female company and doesn't make too many demands on my increasingly less able body.

Later: I am a little disgusted at myself. In rather clipped but still excellent English, the mayor and the chief of police have been showering my ears with somewhat excessive praise regarding my researches into the British folk song; extolling also the importance of a national musical heritage and identity. That's all fine and dandy by me. However, they have taken this as a jumping off point for a filthy tirade against supposedly inferior cultures and societies. Had they forgotten my translations from the *Rig Veda*? Admittedly, certain countries hold the whip hand today, but my feeling is that civilisation goes in geographic cycles and that those enslaved or dubbed 'inferior' will flower in later decades or centuries.

What I did find interesting during the meal with the members of the National Socialist Party – a socialism unrecognisable when compared with our trade union dominated Labour Party back home – was the notion that the Earth is in fact hollow. What was even more intriguing was the preposterous idea that the natural state of matter is ice. Haven't these bigots ever read Einstein or even The Bible? According to the Nazis, the sun and other stars apparently have icy cores. So, in that case, what are they – comets?!

For my own personal safety, I nodded half-drunken agreement, without committing myself verbally. I have always felt that I owed

Germany a debt of gratitude because I used their prisoners of war to write up the scores for *The Planets*, but quite how these duffers have been awarded the Olympics, I swear I do not know!

   - Gustav

I couldn't leave the subject alone. For my next trick, back in 1996-7, having playfully recast Gustav Holst firstly as a 1960s cultural icon I then pictured him going on to become a 1990s elder statesman. From stargazing innovator to assured star of the National Curriculum in but a few decades. Learned theses suggest hidden themes, such as an ongoing search for the 999 names of God. Techno-boffins play his work backwards and at varying unnatural speeds, thus detecting inhuman (some say satanic) influences amid the booming and screeching. Privately, Holst is doubtless dismayed by this nonsensical meddling with his masterpiece but the great man refuses to comment publicly, this side of the Supreme Court judgement.

With such critical standing comes responsibility. A group of philanthropic rock musicians contacts him to elicit his support for the 'Planet Aid' project targeted at alleviating suffering and want down in Asia Minor. His record company floods the market with rumours and spin-off merchandise, all the time pestering him, "Gus, old son, when are you going to write a mega-smash 'Planet Suite II'? We've got mountains of CD-ROM interactive virtual Game Boy tie-ins all ready to roll."

Next up are the environmental campaigners Earthpeace: "Mr Holst, Mr Human Being Holst, we need you to compose a 'Gaia Symphony'. We want you to save the world. Everybody must do their bit."

Even his 'tribute' band, The Solar Holsters, get in on the act. Guitarist and synthesiser player Steve 'Mercury' Blue declares, "Of course, the old Swede-Brit wrote some kicking tunes and we enjoy playing them but wouldn't it be great if he knocked out another 'Joybringer' or 'World in Union', eh?"

*

The Bringer of War

Here comes Mars, distantly at first but put your ear to the ground – his army, his personal killing machine approaches. Bring me my sword of decapitation; bring me my rock and rolling chariots of fire. Let's bomb this place back to the Stone Age.

The Bringer of Peace

Oh Venus! We sit by a placid lake in your heavenly garden of delights. Birds twitter and forest rodents gambol through the clean undergrowth. Walt Disney has eradicated tooth and claw and we shall live forever in a drawn Eden.

The Winged Messenger

Hurry! This one's from the man upstairs to the missionary woman below... and this next mercurial missive is a paper chain linking hands across the ocean, cultures across the ether. Hurry up please, it's Greenwich Mean Time.

The Bringer of Jollity

There is a conflict here: a boyish melody evoking fun and games, pitted against the more stately procession that befits my regal status. Call me Jove, call me Zeus, call me your majesty. Just don't call me Ishmael.

The Bringer of Old Age

Slow, ponderous, pondering. With my wrinkle rings I represent respected age. But beware the Saturnalia, the month of change when slave becomes master and old becomes young. I shall throw off the shackles and proclaim, "I exist!"

The Magician

I coupled with my Earth Mother and produced countless children until one ungrateful son removed my Uranian testicles. Still, when you've got necromancy, who needs sex? So long as that Mickey Mouse doesn't come along to mess up my brooms and potions.

The Mystic

A calm trickle of notes signals my late entrance. I am blue like the ocean. Female voices praise me wordlessly.

I'm really missing the school and the college, particularly the twin fires of creativity and occasional dissent thrown at me by the not so genteel students. With a few notable exceptions, most professional musicians are boring automatons, doing what is necessary to interpret the sheet music but reserving the bulk of their energies for new methods of instant inebriation or unusual chat up lines to use on chorus girls. Still, I can't play the high and mighty moral king as my raven-haired soprano, Jane Weill, waits to share my slumber this very evening. I shall miss her when the tour finally ends. We have a few engagements to fulfil when we return to England: smaller scale seaside and end of the pier shows at Brighton, Shiplea and so forth.

I have felt very close to death lately. Although much of my work has been based on or influenced by the primitive religious and astrological beliefs of earlier cultures, my basic Christian faith remains undiminished.

In intellectual circles, there is much talk these days of the death of God. I will have none of it. The question is, has always been and always will be, not is there a God, but what is His nature or form?

I may soon be blessed with an answer.

– Gustav

*

"...You see, like, Gustav Holst, he's the guvnor, man, you know what I mean? He was there on the case before anyone else. Forget your Byrds, your Hawkwind and your Pink Floyd, yeah? He was space rock before there was rock and before there was space. Respect the man."

Sun and Moon

⊙ ☾

And it came to pass that the Sun and the Moon became lovers. Those who had anticipated this assignation smiled on the inevitability of such a union. The Sun was regal, courtly and attentive in his somewhat old-fashioned way. The Moon received his favours with her womanly grace and charm, but it should not be assumed that she was lacking in spirit or was in any way the weaker half of this heavenly partnership. They rolled together like gold and silver.

Alas, there were some doubters who felt that the man and the woman were too unalike to make a lasting success of the match – he with his overpowering devotion and constancy, she with her feminine wiles and her hidden side. Sad to tell, their fiery ardour cooled after a time. He wanted everything intense and undiminished every second of the day. She found that at times she loved him fully with all her heart but at other times her feelings faded to virtual invisibility. Even so, the passion was oft rekindled.

On separating, they looked deep into their own nature and divided their possessions thus: the Sun being such a regular guy would have charge of the day and the year. The Moon with her unhappy reputation for being fickle would take charge of the night and the month. She was welcome to join her ex during the day whenever the mood took her. The Earth was his to warm; the sea was hers to rile and soothe. He would mark age, she would guard menstruation.

They'd treated the whole divorce business as mature adults.

Even so, the passion would be oft rekindled.

Cometh the Comet

Comet Wylie was discovered by Earth's astronomers as it crossed the elliptical plane of Jupiter. Picking up debris from the asteroid belt, it sped on towards Mars the red planet, causing some perturbation in the orbits of Deimos and Phobos and itself having its sunward loop knocked slightly out of true. Experts ran computer simulations; scientists made calculations and predictions. Religious authorities spoke out. Everyone had an opinion but the broad consensus was that the irregular ball of ice and dust and its attendant vaporous tail was 99.9% certain to hit Earth with catastrophic consequences. It could be like the death of the dinosaurs all over again as megatons of dirt, crust, volcanic gases, superheated water vapour and the like were thrown into the atmosphere by its Atlantean impact. The world might be dark for decades, shrouded in the comet's funereal cloud. The weather system might never properly recover.

"Something must be done," insisted the broadsheets.

"Nuke The Bastard!" screamed the tabloids.

The United Nations Security Council passed the problem over to the world's richest military regime. The American President gave the go-ahead for a battery of modified Cruise missiles to be trained on the moving target. Launch Day couldn't come too soon as the 'Killer Comet' continued its inexorable progress. There would be just this one chance for a direct hit or at the very least a glancing shot which would alter the visitor's course.

During the modification process, however, an informal alliance of disaffected desk-bound servicemen, high school computer hackers and a leading Greenpeacenik had interfered with the lead rocket's guidance system so that number one missile and its five cohorts took a right turn that should have been a slight deviation to the left and all the phallic weapons set off in the direction of Pluto.

The culprits were quickly identified and summarily executed. It was too late, however, for a second round of shots as ionised debris would undoubtedly pepper the upper atmosphere with potentially disastrous results. It was time for Plan B.

Captains of industry, ministers of state, top-earning entertainers, hands that rocked the cradle of trade... some vanished surreptitiously, others with high-security ceremoniousness. Top-line workers in new technologies, hydroponics and genetics followed in the second class carriages as the nuclear bunkers rapidly filled. Average estimates suggested a necessary underground period of fifty years before the Earth was fit for fat cats and celebrities to walk abroad again. This was the last many of our glorious leaders would see of sun and star light. These were the last few days of anything for the billions of plebeians, wage slaves and middle managers they'd left behind. There were riots, unsuccessful attacks on known bunker sites and innumerable outbreaks of abject panic. The comet could now be seen on any five-dollar telescope from the local clearance store. There was time for one wild night of death defying carousing on what is variously remembered as The Last Good Friday or World Mardi Gras Day; then, as the comet became visible to the naked, bloodshot eye, a sudden calm descended upon the peoples of Earth.

"Let us die with dignity," was the message from the surviving independent press and electronic media, and this sentiment was readily adhered to across the globe. Men, women and children switched off their PCs, dropped their farming implements or cast aside their begging bowls and gathered on hills and coastlines to watch and wait for inevitable judgement. Many even switched off their i-phones.

Far-distant spectroscopic analyses had erred badly. The comet was huge and magnificent but its bodily mass was more thinly spread than the sky-watching scientists had predicted. It caught in the Earth's gravitational field but failed to descend as feared. Rather, it hung in the heavens, a fiery cone visible over the twilight time. Comet Wylie became a companion to the sun setting and the moon rising. The millions saved from its expected fury observed it with awe, reverence and lingering trepidation.

It is not recorded who first dubbed the new satellite 'God's Finger' but the label caught the popular imagination and a change came over the behaviour of the meek inheritors of the Earth. Nation traded unto nation with peace in their hearts. A culture of contemplation and shared insights replaced the Darwinian battle for survival and dominance. And up above hung the celestial digit: a warning, an admonishment, but also a reminder that He was still around keeping guard over Humankind's affairs.

It was decided to further incarcerate the cowards and reprobates who'd taken to the bunkers by building gigantic stone monoliths and limestone pyramids atop their hiding places. Concrete the bastards inside their luxury tombs; let's see if those wasters can ever chisel their way out of that mausoleum!

Over time, a surge in sunspot activity meant that the ice in the comet's nucleus gradually condensed into pure showers and brilliant rainbows. As the new temples went up to celebrate this further miracle, so 'God's Finger' faded from sight, although many still looked in the old quadrant and thought they saw it long after all traces had melted away into the ecosphere. Nevertheless, the advent of the comet had heralded an unprecedented era of peace and stability. It was not paradise but it was three steps closer.

Until a new clique of leader types began to emerge.

The Saturn Alias

♄

The differences between this world and our own are not so great as our philosophers and financiers had hoped. Certainly there is a marked absence of smog, grime and Earth's ever present noise and light pollution, but those anticipating a pre, or even post-industrial Eden are going to be sorely disappointed. For myself, I have become a tad lackadaisical, as if the completion of a journey dismissed by many of my compatriots as pure conjecture has left me satiated.

Our months of training had fostered the necessary team spirit that would enable us to withstand the slow elliptical crawl through the emptiness to the opposite side of the sun without descending into barbarism or fanaticism. Lord knows there were many other recruits physically fitter and intellectually more capable than our motley band but the support staff had the foresight to seek balance above all other attributes when selecting the crew of The Narcissus. By now I almost believe that I grew up with these people, from Captain Jane Wylie to maverick engineer Wild Jack. I would even go so far as to feel that we have been together in previous lives, although this remains mostly a dream state impression and cannot be verified by fact or research.

There was always some parent or responsible adult further up the beach in a striped deckchair whenever we children ventured onto the sand. Or at least there was meant to be. It might be Jack's parents with their cans of supermarket beer and last week's scandal rags; it might be Dutch Uncle Nicholas with his grimy monocle and mysterious star charts.

I was five, close friends with Jane, not realising just how futile the future search would be because the one I sought had shown so early. Staying with her would be the problem.

We were making a four-turret castle with crumbly walls and a moat whose wet sand kept drinking my buckets of brine. We were so close and easy with each other in the manner that happy children can often be. Sometimes we picked up conversations from two or three days ago, as if our whole lives were one pre-determined totality.

Out of the blue, I announced, "Dutch Uncle Nicholas told me there's as many stars in the sky as there are drops of water in the ocean."

At the age of a mere half a decade she replied, "Let's do an experiment and see. You can tip your bucket really carefully and I'll count. I can count to a hundred, you know. Mummy taught me."

Four years further on, bored with the beach, chewing a blade of grass on the cliff top, she would answer, "I don't like Dutch Uncle Nicholas. He makes me feel all funny."

At sweet sixteen, she'd suggest, "Let's fill up with home brew. Those buckets will do."

At twenty-something – or more – it's just me on my own, answering my own question with a dismissive tirade: "Scientists! Think they know everything. Prove that the universe is really expanding! Prove that there's more than we can see! Show me that it's not merely another series of distorted reflections... Bring her back to me!"

And now I'm rocketed back here to present time, conjuring memories into actuality...

Jane's at the other end of the beach. I'm surprised to spot her. She hasn't recognised me. There are two young children with her, doubtless the magnets drawing her to the waves and the rock pools. I know one of the youngsters is definitely her offspring; I hope the other is merely a kindergarten friend.

I won't speak to her today. Unless she sees me...

But she's guarding her charges and I'm maintaining my distance.

*

... Eighteen now.

"I'm marrying Jeremy," she said.

"You can't! I mean, why? And what about us?"

"Simon, it's friendship with us, that's all. It's not going any further."

"You don't have to marry him."

"Live with him, set up house with him, go round the world with him, share a sleeping bag with him... Simon, it amounts to the same thing."

"I thought ... we... "

"But you never really showed it. Except maybe that time on the cliff. Other times… You couldn't close the gap. It just didn't work out between us; not in a boyfriend-girlfriend way. Oh, you know what I mean."

I received my papers of exile with good grace. I signed up with the Heliocentric Exploratory Corps and made several circuits of the solar system, acquiring a degree, dozens of short lived jobs and experiencing a few ultimately unfulfilling encounters with the alien species Young Urban Female. And now I've reached that clichéd point in every space jockey's career when the view screen turns back towards Homesville. Specifically, Shiplea Beach.

She had her husband, her home, her child or children and her part-time job like a complex ring system warding off potential invaders. But I was selfish, even self-destructive, and determined to re-establish old friendships – or reopen old wounds.

*

13 Lines on Saturn

SATURN IS spinning askew like all the best El Dorados.

SATURN IS riven by contrary winds. Crack thy cheeks and a-way, hey, we'll blow the man down.

SATURN IS banded like a rubber ball.

SATURN IS flattened at the poles so would be unlikely to bounce true.

Even so, SATURN IS more regular than its gassy neighbour Jupiter.

SATURN WAS Galileo's last vision before the eternal abyss.

SATURN IS surrounded by thousands of minuscule rings, each in its own imperfect orbit around the equator.

SATURN IS stabilised by their presence – or else is being slowly imprisoned. As this latter process could take billions of years, we're unlikely to witness its completion.

The SATURN V rocket, which helped launch Neil and Buzz to the Moon, is still one of the most powerful weapons ever constructed.

SATURN IS associated with the devil, the goat and the horned one in popular mythology.

SATURN IS the guiding planet for the star sign of Capricorn. Famous Capricornians include Jesus Christ and Jane Wylie.

In Babylonian times, the dozen days of the SATURNALIA saw slave become master and a whole society indulge in a bout of unbridled bacchanalia. In the Christian hegemony this has been watered down to a partridgely twelve days of Christmas.

By common consent, SATURN IS the crown jewel of the solar system.

I suppose there must have been times during my adolescence when for a few days or weeks our gang achieved the necessary balance between study expectations and the world changing passion associated with the teenage mind. For all the obsession with legal, illegal and frequently antisocial kicks, we had our idealistic moments, too. Homework would be completed quickly or skipped entirely so that a dozen of us could combine the wisdom of our sheltered lives within the welcoming confines of the Pier Cafe or The King's Head pub – so long as we drank nothing stronger than shandy. When we weren't feuding with the reputedly posher kids along the coast in Chesilham, we'd catch the bus to their fleapit cinema which screened three-month-old art house productions to a mixed crowd of students and the sozzled, at fifteen minutes past Saturday closing time. We generally walked back under an ultramarine sky splotched with stars and galactic spittle. It would be three in the morning with Jack worried about getting up for his delivery job in Overstrand and Alison whinging that her mother would kill her.

"Not before she sniffs your underwear," Eddie commented lasciviously.

One summer, the Chesilham Roxy ran a series of science fiction films: *2001, Forbidden Planet, Alien Terror in Nantucket County* and so on. With the added attraction of de rigueur red and green 3D glasses for several old 50s flicks, we soaked up a bundle of movies about alien pods, killer bugs, tin can spacecraft and general paranoia. There was one film, directed by Gerry 'Thunderbirds' Anderson, I think, which postulated the scientific impossibility of a parallel Earth on the opposite of the sun. Initially, it was Philip and Alison who were most taken with this idea and, as these things do, the preposterous notion became a talking point amongst our group for weeks on end. Supposing everything there was exactly the same and in sync with us on Earth number one?

"If it's a mirror image," suggested Rachel, "maybe those of us who are girls here are boys there and vice versa."

"You kinky cow," said Joe.

"I always wondered about you," Bill added.

Whilst she was busy slapping their heads and attempting to gouge slivers of skin from their hostile faces, I adopted her theory. Thinking aloud, I commented, "In that case, you could travel to the other Earth to fall in love with yourself. You wouldn't need friends, you'd just hang around with your duplicate or female twin or whatever, do everything or be idle together."

Jane smiled. "We should call the mythical planet Narcissus."

There was full agreement about this. Jack, in an unusually academic mood, put forward the idea of writing a detailed history and social report on the mirror world as part of our English Literature option but everybody else was understandably against this. The last thing we wanted was to destroy the magic of this shared notion by rendering it into a school project.

For a month or two, we began referring to Narcissus whenever two or more of us met socially. The place was as real as Shiplea or Chesilham and yet also the repository of hopes and dreams in the manner of an El Dorado or Shangri-La.

Hush-hush, top secret, old bean. Mention the haven to no one. If word does slip out, swear blind you have no idea how to get there.

Apart from Eddie, who was sure to enrol in the Anglian Regiment the moment he escaped the sixth form, we were pacifists to a man and a woman.

As Jane put it, "If the military ever find out about Narcissus, they'll start an interplanetary conflict."

"That's right," Rachel concurred. "They'll have found the perfect excuses to unite all the countries of this world under a gigantic dictatorship in order to wage war against the impostors."

Silently, I continued to worry that the parallel Earth was out of sync with our home planet. Supposing they were a hundred years behind us and still relying on horse or steam power. They'd have no chance against our split atoms and computer guided projectiles. Then again, if they were a century ahead of us and we got them riled like a swarm of bees...

The existence of Narcissus was a conceit which briefly sustained all of us for several weeks. Mere wish-fulfilment on the part of we Shiplea Seasiders, of course. Typically, I clung to the concept for much longer than my colleagues. I spent many a wet afternoon sketching Narcissus beach scenes complete with a crescent moon and a baleful Saturn hanging judgementally in the washed-out sky. I nicked most of the ideas from the Bruce Pennington backdrops on the covers of old sci-fi paperbacks by A. E. Van Vogt, Frank Herbert and the like, wishing fervently that I could breathe life into the scantily clad maidens who also adorned these tomes.

Narcissus existed because we created it. The mirror planet was a necessity of our needs and desires.

"The currently held belief, of course, students, is that space is curved. If you could look acutely enough and for long enough you would eventually be able to see the back of your head... in front of you!"

One of the girls giggled nervously at Mr Holkham's suggestion but others snorted. Jack scribbled on the inside cover of his notebook, "I could use two mirrors to do that."

Jane raised her hand and politely enquired, "But what's all this got to do with T. S. Eliot?"

Old Hocus-Pocus flicked a glance at the heavens and answered, "Beginnings and ends, my dear. Eliot is talking about both the personal and the universal. Do you not see that?"

"Not without two mirrors," interrupted Jack in an over-loud stage whisper.

"You students have got to see beyond the literature," Holkham continued.

"What – like to the back of our heads?" asked Philip.

Hocus-Pocus shook his greying mane and mumbled the usual despairing words about the younger generation. Simon stopped sucking his pen long enough to suggest, "But to see that far you'd have to live forever... or at least twelve billion years or so."

Holkham smiled. "At least one of you loafers can use his brain," he commented.

"Bloody boffin!" was Jack's retort. "Going home to fiddle with your telescope, Simey?"

The teacher and the accused let the outburst pass. Revision time was slipping away like the light from a fading star. Everyone was approaching several gees of stress and pressure. In the first mirror lurked *The Four Quartets, Romeo and Juliet,* the migraine inducing *Lyrical Wit of the Seventeenth Century* and the 1,000 page trawl through *Middlemarch.* The second beckoning mirror held the more alluring teenage concerns of alcohol, weed, pills, pranks and sex, sex, sex. Quite how anyone was supposed to sit down to three hours of study every night was as insoluble a question as, 'Is God dead or is He sleeping?'

On top of which, the Chesilham Fair started this Saturday and even if you didn't go on any rides or throw darts at the stalls you had to show up just to be seen in numbers by your deadly rivals from along the coast. A-Levels...? May devils! If you didn't know the stuff by now you sure as hell wouldn't hit upon it during next month's exam.

We had known each other forever. We huddled together under animal skins in the freezing caves of the Palaeolithic. We crawled, waddled and slithered through the swamps of the Carboniferous. We were single celled yet aching for complexity in the amniotic seas. Life after life we would never let ourselves be torn asunder.

There were all the films I'd seen, the books I'd read and the snippets of meaningful conversation amid word mountains of land filling drivel. Sometimes what I'd imagined were fresh ideas was just regurgitation, lumps of thoughts that simply wouldn't disappear down the waste disposal. But at other times I was certain my notions contained, if not an entirety, then at least a modicum of originality. It was important to my ego to feel this. Mozart, Shakespeare, Descartes, Dutch Uncle Nicholas ... they all held a huge amalgam of their many and various influences and antecedents yet were able to stamp their own brand or originality into their philosophic art. Me, too, please God!

I dabbled in astrology for a while at college, encouraged no doubt by the vain hope of bedding some henna-haired, flower-skirted handmaiden of mysterious fortune. I retain some faith in its basic tenets, although my infatuation for the local female chart-caster quickly faded. My long-term thoughts return to Jane Wylie. Her ruling planet is, of course, the oh-so appropriate semi-precious orb of Saturn. Like the planet, she is be-ringed: in her case, with a husband, children, work, a mortgage, family crises and a hundred and one other worldly cares. And yet all objects in the solar system are theoretically within reach.

Her husband does not deserve her. Whatever she saw in him ten or twelve or however many years ago will have faded by now, or have been revealed as a cruel illusion all along. Even if possession is nine-tenths or more of any law, the bottom line is: I'm back in town and I mean business.

I wish I felt as sure of myself as I try to sound. I've tried that old psychological trick of 'visualising', picturing how we're going to meet up, link up, stay solid, but… Several of my conjectured scenarios have very downbeat endings. Even when I imagine us together I know that, realistically, our relationship will be intermittent at best – snatched moments of clarity against the eternal background radiation.

Naturally, there are other choices open to me if I could only be bothered to see them or seek them. For the moment, I'm settled back into lodgings in Shiplea. I have collected the last of my (too) many belongings from London. Old toys, old comics, lemon and sugar memories and mementoes. Spreading them out on the duvet in front of me, I still get a bit of a buzz and am transported back to the ancient sunshine, feeling just how I did back then as a kid or a teenager. Yet it's all something of a Virtual Reality trip compared to the real experience.

I could phone her… keep walking past her house… watch and wait for the inevitable make or break.

Or else, as St Paul said, maybe it is time to put away childish things.

*

It was nearly July. I had a few weeks temporary terminal with a half promise of a permanent post in September, but either way no income for August. The kids weren't into working too hard so I was simply keeping them ticking over with maths and language revisions and a few team games when the Head wasn't looking.

In the evenings, I had re-familiarised myself with Shiplea, not that anywhere had changed markedly during my decade of absence. My childhood home – sold too cheaply by my mother prior to emigration – had degenerated into a ramshackle three-up-two-down with rubbish overflowing the bins, a half naked teenage boy leering precariously at passers-by from an upstairs window and a decidedly rough looking dog shitting on the front lawn. Maybe I was being too snobbish, maybe this had always been the least salubrious street in town.

I had also walked past the real focus of my hopes on almost every early nocturnal ramble. On one occasion Jane's mother was pruning the hedgerow. She failed to recognise me and I could not summon the courage to speak to her and ask what I needed to ask. Pathetic. Thirty years old, veteran of several sticky moments in London pubs and on demonstrations, and I couldn't open my mouth to politely question a middle-aged lady about her wayward daughter, my one, my only, my truly...

This class was the usual mix of head cases, sad cases and the genuinely pleasant. We'd been mostly studying the Ancient Greeks, although it was with the geography curriculum in mind that I took them off to the beach last week. We duly collected a few coffee jars of sand and cliff samples. Some of the more enterprising had brought their own spades and began digging the usual mound with a moat while the others munched crisps or dared the sea to get their shoes wet. I was worrying a little that they weren't particularly taking to the myths and the history when suddenly one of the boys suggested they build a labyrinth rather than a castle... and then one of the girls amended the idea to a labyrinth under a castle. Instantly, a mixed group of ten set about constructing tunnels and turnings and blind alleys and a concealed lair. The castle atop was eventually raised and displaced to the western side. The rest of the class watched or helped as necessary – fetching water or strands of seaweed – and the finished model was quite magnificent. We hastily put up makeshift notices asking people not to disturb our artwork and marked the whole thing off with a stone circle. I suspect many of my pupils slept with fingers crossed that night. I detoured in the morning and neither tide nor trampling had damaged the Cretan palace. We made clay models of all the participants and their boats; we wrote stories, drew pictures, acted out the drama in miniature on the beach. It was a magical three days. I had the presence of mind to take a few photos before both Ben and Chloe, the acknowledged brains crew of Burgundy class, decided the model had served its purpose and at an unseen signal encouraged everyone to kick it to pieces. I didn't interfere.

The flint circle is still there, a mystery younger than time and less controversial than Stonehenge.

Narcissus is turning out to be the world of our dreams.

We have been well received by the local inhabitants. Unlike our stalagmited continents, their world has one huge land mass surrounded by a great swathe of blue ocean. Our new friends simply smile when we insist that we have travelled back to Gondwanaland. Seasonal changes are as subtle as the first star of twilight. We are encamped as pampered guests on the outskirts of one of their larger cities. I would describe the climate as Mediterranean, if such a sea ever existed here. Thoughts of incompatibility have been swiftly banished by succulent offerings of fruit, drowsy wine and tactile companionship.

My passion for our captain, the indisputable Jane Wylie, remains undiminished, but there are... temptations.

The whole scenario takes my thoughts back to a boyhood spent on the beach at Shiplea. Doubtless, the truly hot, still summer days only amounted to half a dozen or so each year, but in memory they seem numberless.

It was a family friend, the flawed genius Dutch Uncle Nicholas, who first suggested, in modern times at least, that what we thought of as the radio songs of immensely distant stars were in fact surface distortions and echoes from the barrier enclosing the solar system. A Lewis Carroll of the late twentieth century, his misdemeanours meant that his pioneering work became obscured by the more highly publicised findings of his followers; and, sadly, overshadowed by sordid revelations regarding his personal life.

Astronomy is the only vital science to humankind; everything else is subservient.

There has been some understandable commotion about Naughty Nick's theory that our heliocentric family may be all there is, as opposed to the previously held dogma of an ever expanding and well-nigh infinite universe. In layman's terms: If we can never even contemplate the colonisation of worlds around other stars – because there are no worlds around the so-called stars, which themselves don't really exist – then once we finally foul up the Earth with our pillage and plunder and global warming, we're fucked.

We are not yet at the stage of absolute proof for the new heresy. What is clear, however, is that there appears to be more to our heat source and its little circle of planets than was previously imagined. As our own flight has demonstrated, the world-count need not end at nine, or eight for those who discount Pluto.

Jane Wylie has called an emergency crew meeting. I arrive a little late, just in time to hear her muscle-bound brother Eddie proclaim, "All I said was that shipwrecking ourselves here might prove to be a futile gesture. Earth will only take a year or two to mount another expedition."

"That's as may be," our captain mutters. "We can only live moment to moment, as we have always done."

"The future we live is never the one anticipated," I offer as a supportive axiom.

Jane smiles. I am momentarily rewarded. She continues, "Jeremy has already shut down transmissions."

"They might decide we've experienced technical difficulties or they might conclude something unforeseen and fatal has befallen us," he explains.

He squeezes Jane's hand. They have been sharing a contour couch for several months now.

"They won't be scared off," Eddie argues. "We're not safe here forever."

"That's not the point," Jane insists. "Do you really want this place opened up to the multinational asset strippers, the career politicians and…" – she pauses for effect – "…estate agents?" Sooner or later there must come a choice like this for all explorers, physical, poetic and conjectural. T.S. Eliot said something about arriving home and knowing the place for the first time. Robert Louis Stevenson never returned from the South Seas.

Authoritatively, she says, "I move that we sabotage the mission. All in favour?"

The vote is unexpectedly unanimous.

It's easy to believe in the entropic notion of the universe, easy to accept that everything is moving – even rushing – away from everything else. Most of life seems to consist of a succession of major losses. All the certainties of childhood – family, friends, notions of stability and stasis – gradually decay and die. Attempting to offset these amputations, one acquires a string of material possessions of doubtful value. We reach out and grab a few lifeless satellites or rings around ourselves while the stars flicker and fade out.

Forever.

We meet. There is that smile. A talk about youthful times. Another talk. A fleeting holding of hands. Maybe I get invited back as a much-missed, old-time teenage and childhood companion to meet her children, her darling husband, her matching chairs and sofa…

I become a regular visitor. Or else, we dog each other's footsteps, arranging chance encounters that froth with delighted grins and shared confidences. She can get away for a few hours, meet me somewhere, see me on my own, our own. We rekindle a friendship that once seemed indissoluble. We become lovers. We snatch what time together we can grasp without bringing our whole other lives crashing to the ground.

We remain lovers, snatching moments that ought to have been lifetimes. It is enough to sustain.

For now.

From: The Anglian Examining Board English Literature A-Level Paper

Read *13 Lines on Saturn*. Write an essay discussing both the qualities and shortcomings of this prose poem. Within your answer bear in mind issues such as: the repetitive format of each discrete section; the scientific knowledge demonstrated by the author; and whether the snippets of mythological and astrological detail spoil or enhance the piece. Remember also to always pay attention to conventional English spelling and grammar.

You should allow thirty-five minutes for this question.

Helios

Inspired by reading several cranky South American philosophers, Dutch Uncle Nicholas had recently set about his 'Great New Scheme'. Initial intentions to build a full-scale model of the universe were eventually muted into a representation of the solar system. At first, his several young charges were rather taken with the idea, as it seemed to give them licence to run mad circles around Shiplea beach or the cliff top car park. When the professor tried to impose a proper order on proceedings, his spiralling planets and cartwheeling satellites became space refusniks and the whole creation fell victim to unpredictable entropy. A temporary restoration was only achieved by promises of future candy flosses and dodgem rides next month when the funfair came to town.

Eventually Mars and Venus wandered off into the salty spray and Jupiter began a solitary spitting competition on the shingles. The dissatisfied astronomer blamed himself for the children's loss of interest. Maybe he'd been wrong to even think of cutting corners. In order to make a faithful replica of the heliocentric universe he would need to make his model at least actual size, if not, in fact, bigger than the real thing so as to adequately demonstrate sub-molecular relationships and the like.

"Children! Children!" he called. "Can you just come and help me once more?"

But there were stones to skim, starfish to tease and toes to turn blue-white with cold salinity. The whole group ignored the old man, except for Jack's mocking index finger tapped against his forehead.

"Children," Dutch Uncle Nicholas implored, "come back, please! I only want you to be yourselves!"

Her mother kept telling her that she had more than enough on her plate with her studies and her Saturday job and a regular string of suitors. Why suffer the tribulations of being a muse-audience-shoulder-to-cry-on to some upstart, weedy little, seventeen-year-old poet? But Simon was a friend of long standing and, "Anyway, Mother, he's not weedy!"

"He's not much of a poet, either, girl!"

The last was maybe true but at least Simon wasn't as irredeemably macho as her brother Eddie, the self-styled Jupiter, and his proto-Jovian gang. Or maybe Simon had just realised earlier than most men – complete babies, all of them! – that there was more to life than fist fights, explosive action films and getting pissed every night.

Now he was in her bathroom readying himself for a reading at the local pub. He was probably nicking all her talcum powder and deodorant – such babies; no, really! He'd left his notebook open on the sofa. Jane had carte blanche to look at all of his scribbling, even the coded missives she suspected were declarations of affection for her.

She read, "In His first incarnation, God was a painter, sowing the seeds of Chiaroscuro, a monochrome minimalist working on an epic scale -"

"I'm ready," he interrupted. "Let's go out to play."

"Yes," said Jane, hurtled back to being five years old again, "let's go out to play. But Mummy told me not to get my dress wet."

"We can build sand models."

"And stone ones. I'm good at them."

"Betcha I'm better."

He was such a typical little boy with his red trunks and his short blond hair. A perfectionist even at a mere half a decade, he always liked to wash his pebbles before placing them in a picture. It didn't make too much difference because the Sun dried them faded or colourless. The walk to and from the water with his plastic bucket gave Simon time to think. At just a handful of years old, he liked to think.

"What are you making, Jane?"

"The Gingerbread House."

"Again?"

"Yes, again. Why not?"

"Don't cry, Jane. I like this new one better. You've done it really, really good. I'm making the solar system."

"The what?"

"The Sun, Moon and planets and stuff. I saw it in a book by Dutch Uncle Nicholas. Did you know the Sun's in the middle?"

"Everybody knows that, stupid!"

"They didn't till twenty hundred years ago or something. Anyway, I've got to concentrate."

She took a quizzical, feminine look at his square yard of beach. "What's that big stone?"

"That's Jupiter. It's got red spots like the measles all over it."

"I thought that was Mars. An' where's Saturn?"

"The next one. I don't know how to do the rings. Should I use little stones or just draw them in the sand?"

"You could walk backwards around it three times. That's a magic spell, that is."

"Of course," he said, his voice deeper, older, sadder, broken, back to being seventeen and dressed now in his 'urban troubadour' outfit of brushed cotton trousers and grey unbuttoned shirt, "it's a little known fact that all planets have a ring system, visible or otherwise. Neptune has one. Jupiter's got a dark one. The discovery hasn't officially been announced yet."

"And what about Earth?"

"Apart from the space junk – you know, dead satellites and all that – we've got the Van Allen radiation belts. Like I said, all planets have got rings. To keep them in orbit properly, like stabilisers on a bicycle. Or to help protect them from the slings and arrows of outrageous misfortune."

She brushed at his tears with her pointed fingers. She was sorry the gig hadn't gone well, but what did he expect? She kissed him once on the forehead, sisterly fashion, because there was her secret fiancé Jeremy to think about and she didn't want to become embroiled in a misread situation with Simon.

"I'm sorry your show went badly," she whispered. "It was the audience, not your poetry..."

From Fast Eddie Wylie's Five Minute Guide to the Galaxy

Since the days of Darwin there have been many attempts to square the opposing circles of evolutionary history and divine creation. At this time of turbulence there are several theories vying for acceptance. Many commentators have lately cast doubt upon the Big Bang prognosis and its attendant notion of an infinite but expanding universe. Indeed, in these difficult days, the focus has shifted back to a heliocentric point of view – there is the solar system and nothing else; all contradictory data comes from distorted reflections off the barrier somewhere beyond Pluto (ah, but what lies outside this bubble, you may well inquire?).

This 'Creed of Helios' has gained respectability with the united opposition parties, the Modern Moderate Alliance, whose motto 'This far but no further' finds an astronomical extrapolation in heliocentrism. The controlling forces of the British Normality Patrol have yet to pronounce on an authorised version of the birth of the universe and such silence is perceived by the more liberal observers as a slight chink in their populist armour.

The mid-1990s saw the (apparent) discovery of other planets orbiting nearby stars. Religious opportunists took this as a sign of God hedging His bets. So what if the solar system was no longer so unique? In any half-decent scientific experiment you'd have several test tubes on the go, then sit back for a few billion years to watch and wait.

Perhaps the most interesting proposal to emerge in recent years has come from the William Herschel Institute for the Advancement of Music. Put simply, both evolution and seven-day creation are correct.

God set the clock of natural selection ticking several hundred million years ago, took off on a galactic sojourn and on His return decided matters weren't moving ahead fast enough. The Evolve Programme was summarily scrapped and the exhausting but effective Quick Creation Option was taken. Our constituent molecules, however, still retain the memory of the long crawl out of the primeval slime.

Jane's husband was away on business. I'd agreed to meet her on the beach just down from the pier. Her little boy was splashing in the waves, unconcerned that his pink toes were turning first bloodless white then refrigerator blue. There's a myth that people who live at the seaside never go in the sea. We do, but not when the holidaymakers are looking.

I remembered walking along this very gravel thousands, maybe even a million years ago. This was before Jane had mothered any children either with me or anyone else from the tribe. Her features then were less delicate, more hirsute. Everybody's features were less delicate; it was that stage of evolution. In those days she was known as Keeper of the Flame, but I'd seduced her away from the hearth fire onto a quest for a new homeland. A new Eden, or maybe even the original one.

"Simon, don't look so pensive," she said.

"I'm just thinking. Remembering."

"When? Oh, not that time you brought the telescope onto the beach and wanted to tell everyone about the recent transit of Mars through Capricorn or something – "

" – And your annoying brother kicked sand into the tubing and I couldn't get it to focus properly. Actually," I concluded, "I'd conveniently forgotten all that until now. I was going back even further."

"Concentrate on the now," she advised, one eye on me and one on her frolicking son. I smiled. She added, "I'm glad you got out of London. Things seem pretty wild there at the moment."

"It's not so bad if you've got a beard," I answered. "Or a blue sash or something."

She stroked my chin with a rare public display of affection.

My name in prehistoric times was Sky Watcher. A dreamer even then! I'd finally found the courage to stand up to One Fur and his cronies and now my reward was to be trudging the moonlit beach with a badly balanced fish spear in one hand and a Martian canal of cuts in the other. Already my archetype was mapping out a future, a new settlement in these tempestuous climes. Maybe the cold grey waters would offer up boundless meals of fin and scale. Maybe the root vegetables and the yellow blades could be coaxed into growing more plentifully.

I'm not sure my forward-thinking ancestor would appreciate how his modern descendant has turned out. It seems I'm obsessed with recapturing what I almost had in the past, hovering like an unstable satellite around my childhood haunts and my childhood love.

From Hieronymus Herschel's Musical Guide to the Solar System, Argentina, 1988

The Gulong people of the South Pacific have a creation myth in which the god Iapetu courts the goddess Aphrosia under the benevolent eye of their father the Sun. Iapetu creates the Earth as a pretty marble of blue and white. Aphrosia tires of the bauble and sends it spinning carelessly between the light and the dark realms of her celestial parents. Her suitor separates the land from the sea to give pleasing contrasts; the contrary maiden creates winds and clouds and mixes the elements up over and over again. Iapetu then makes bold to offer her the planet Saturn as a huge stoned wedding ring. Aphrosia leaves the gift untended and in a fit of dismay at the apparently endless courtship takes out her wrath on the then fifth planet Pentavir, destroying it in order to create for herself an asteroid belt of chastity.

To date, the betrothal remains in abeyance.

Quite how a primitive people with no concept of distance, difference and ground glass were able to construct such an elaborate metaphor to explain their own existence is just one of many anthropological mysteries that are usually 'explained' by the catch-all, neo-Atlantean 'Lost Knowledge of the Ancients' poppycock so popular with the younger generation.

The planets are subtly shifting their position every second. My horoscope is out of date before I've finished reading it. Flux is the natural order.

Or maybe that means there is no natural order. The whole universe is merely an aftershock from an unimaginably cataclysmic explosion billions of years ago and we've got to expect to be thrown around a bit until things calm down.

As a child I was accustomed to seeing a great expanse of sky. My mother instructed me early in cliff safety as a parental compromise to my independent, investigative spirit. Sometimes I'd stand and watch the weather hurtling across the North Sea towards our oft-battered town. The cloud formations were huge scowling abstracts by angry, bearded Zeus which would arrive in Wagnerian splendour and deposit their burden in atonal percussion all the way inland towards the bubbling Broads and the factory farms. Other times it would drizzle all day – a weekend, or a school holiday, say – and after a surfeit of snakes and ladders, backlog letters to relatives and brain-death TV, I'd stand by my bedroom window for apparent hours looking up at the grey bowl all around me. At last I'd see a glimpse of blue, the hope that greeted the sufferers on the Ark, and sooner than one could honestly expect there would be a broad swathe of joyful colours out to the west. Within a few blinks, the sky would be awash with the reds, yellows and deep roses of a saline sunset. We called it a 'Shiplea evening' and even if I had no reason to go out or was taking a wild detour to buy milk or chocolate from the furthest nearby grocery, this was the time I always liked to experience that slow walk along the beach, in the calm aftermath.

We had frightening winters, spells of cold like the blade of Brutus coupled with a psychopathic sea always attempting to smash the Victorian pier and the heavy stone promenade. But we had beautiful summers, too: days hot and direct when even the regular breeze would take an occasional rest.

When I went to London I loved that as well: in a different way and despite a constant stream of coughs, colds and breathing difficulties. But Shiplea was my home and I was the partially prodigal son, returned.

The Big Bang postulates an outward, expansive movement. This is not too difficult to accept. Even my sketchy knowledge of human, animal and atomic nature allows for the idea that at one primal moment every actual and potential part of the universe was gathered in one infinitesimal place and this cataclysmic proximity set off the original expulsion whose aftershock we call life. But why was everything squashed into this subatomic space? Who put it all there, doubtless knowing it couldn't last more than three thousandths of a second and the resultant mess would spread out all over the place? What the hell was going on before the Big Bang?

From The Hocus-Pocus Guide to Primitive Peoples by Arthur Holkham (private publication)

The Narcissian people of the Southern Delta have a creation myth in which the universe was originally a mirror of unimaginably great size. This mirror carried the property of reflecting inwards as, of course, nothing else existed without. Time began when their accident prone god E-ed fractured the mirror into an infinite number of pieces all moving away from each other 'faster than the wings of birds, faster even than the beams of the yellow sun ball'. Everything which exists is a fragment of this initial perfection and it is the task of Humankind to assist in the recombination of the original perfect state.

The Southern Delta has long been a haunt for hippies, beatniks and dropouts. These days much of the local income derives from various forms of sex tourism. Clearly, the idea of putting everything back together again has encouraged the 'natives' to indulge their many dubious sexual proclivities. Humpty Dumpty meets rumpy-pumpy.

Tidal currents ensure that for several months of the year the delta is effectively an isolated island. Visitors have noted that the various breeds of domestic animals have an undeniably anthropomorphic look about them.

My father should have been a fisherman.

Listen to the callings of the conch shell and I will make you fishers of men.

Instead, he was a foreman in a factory and when that closed down he was a supervisor in a warehouse. In time, the business went bust so he became an assistant in a fancy goods shop but come September he was back on the dole for the next seven months. So, he settled for becoming a fixture in the local pub with his beer, his newspaper and his hand rolled Golden Virginia.

Such descriptions and details are just the coat hanger rather than the full suit. People – all things – are never the mere surface. As a boy, I wanted his spare change for pocket money or his permission to stay up late or his cigarette-wracked body to join me in chasing a football around a cliff top field. Now I'm as grown as I'll ever be, I wish he were here to share all the secrets of our undoubted masculine misdemeanours. Maybe I'm simply looking for some as yet undiscovered, redeeming talent he might have passed along the bloodline.

*

We like to think we know it all: creation, history, science negating the need for God. Two or more million years of theories and guesswork. As I write, we haven't yet successfully sent people beyond the Earth's gravitational pull – because, face it, even the Moon's within pissing distance. We're Know-it-Alls in a far-flung corner of an unimportant galaxy. Big-brained apes... but still apes.

Part of me wants to rush outwards in excess of light speed, catch up with and ride the crest of the Big Bang's expansion shock wave. Another part of me wants to turn inward, go back in time ever closer to that moment of creation. It must have all started somewhere.

The stargazing, the soul-searching and the seemingly unquenchable desire to be reunited with her white skin... It must have all started somewhere.

It was an evening in early May. When H. G. Wells' great-grandson finally gets round to inventing an open to the public time machine, this is the day I'll go back to and subtly alter. It was too early in the season for swarms of day-trippers and holidaymakers but it was just about time for a smart skinny dip after midnight and live to tell the tale.

I hadn't noticed the subtle composition of our group at first. Me – with my B plusses and ninety per cents – I couldn't see the sea for the salt water. To my mind we were just ten teenagers out for a lark, fuelled by lager, pork scratchings and some foul smelling lawn clippings Joe swore was top quality dope. We left Bill and Rebecca back at the pub, still laughing and smoking and looking into each other's eyes. Phil and Alison left us somewhere along the coast road, walking back to his battered old Volvo ostensibly to drive out to Mundesley and check on his sickly grandma. I knew Alison would settle the indulgent crone upstairs in her iron bed with a pot of tea and some digestives, then she and Phil would fornicate all night on the old dear's sofa. Apart from the car it was the only place they could be alone together.

Then there were six. The penny finally dropped that someone, possibly Joe, had sorted it all out to make five butterfly couples. I knew he was well gone on Linda, and Bob and Sue were already an item: which left, jaw-droppingly, Jane Wylie and me. As we reached the fallow field bordering the cliff path, the other four made some facile excuse about 'torch lit explorations of the beach' and just Jane and I were left. There was a sliver of moonlight and a cool, clear sky. Instinctively, I reached out and clasped her hand, just to let her know that we were two sentient apes hurtling through the frightening galaxy on a ball of rock together. I couldn't see her clearly but I remember exactly the clothes she was wearing: strappy white sandals; a black knee- length pencil-thin skirt which made her walking movements just a tiny bit slow and stuttery; a white silk blouse with double buttons; black cardigan with a red rose design, this thrown carelessly over her shoulders; a blue scarf that had once served her feathery hair now loosely fastened around her neck. I have no recollection of my attire.

The local men – our fathers or uncles – were out fishing on the placid North Sea. Their boats were strings of yellow, white and cream lamps splashed across the calm water as if stolen and dropped after a raid on the pier illuminations. From these we gazed upward at the constellations and God's spittle strung in its meandering milkiness across the night sky.

"That one's the Little Bear," I pointed.

"Yeah? Wondering where its porridge has gone, probably."

I laughed. "I always thought Goldilocks was lucky to get out alive."

"Hmm, yes. Her and Red Riding Hood. Cautionary tales to stifle female curiosity, if you ask me."

"I never saw them that way before. Anyway, the shape's not at all like a bear. More like someone's lost their kite. Some little kid, maybe."

She was shivering a little. She asked me for a cigarette but all I had was dead matches. I didn't really approve of smoking but I didn't want to act the killjoy.

"That one," I continued, "is Cassiopeia."

"Looks more like a 'W'."

"Just needs the 'J' to go with it. We're writing our names in the sky tonight."

"You're really into all this astronomy stuff, aren't you?"

"A bit. But to tell the truth I boned up on it before I came out tonight. Just in case."

'Just in case what?"

"Oh... you know."

'Just in case you were sat here with Jane Wylie," she concluded.

I couldn't tell whether she was smiling or not.

'Well, okay, I'm very interested in creation stories and the theory of the Big Bang and stuff like that," I continued.

"Ah, yes. You were quite impressive at the School Debating Challenge. Better than that Chesilham mob. When was that? Last summer!"

"I didn't realise you'd noticed me then," I mumbled. "We were close friends at infant school, Jane, but..."

We sat silently for a long time. Almost everything of importance in the history of the universe had happened within the first three minutes and here we were taking halves of hours to build bridges across the minuscule expanse of space between us, taking all those aeons even to decide whether we wanted to build a bridge. They'd shifted a little in their easy chairs over the centuries but these were the same cross stars which had blessed or hexed Orpheus and Eurydice, Anthony and Cleopatra, Cathy and Heathcliff...

For the man (all right, callow youth!) it was always the same dilemma: when to make the move and how bold a move to make. To say one or two casual words which might indicate a secondary layer of meaning? To touch accidentally and play off the temperature of the response? To become bestial with only the sight of a crescent moon, to grab and half-ravish and prove one's physical longing for this earthbound angel, to show her the uncontrollable urges she stirred within this masculine breast?

I waited. I did nothing. Not that could be seen, anyhow. My mind projected words, sentiments, images: Jane, I love you; Jane, let's get together as a couple, like this; let's become one celestial mass, with no space separating us...

I waited. I did nothing. Despite all the wishes and fantasies and the arrogant assumption of now – "Oh, yes, I'd go back and be as bold as brass, right enough, old son!" – in spite of all the bravado and all the knowledge even then that this might turn out to be a crucial moment, I cannot change the way I am. I've regularly needed four years just to make friends with someone; how much longer it must take to become a lover, a life companion?

I reached across, took her hand, helped her get to her feet. Her fingers were thin and bony, like my own. One day they might yet wrap together. With all the courage I could muster, or the mustard I could custard, I pressed my lips gently against her right cheek, catching a slightly acidic hint of perfume from her neck and the gossamer caress of her scarf. Then we walked back to the road.

Joe and Linda emerged just a little sheepishly from some undergrowth. Linda's hair was dishevelled and Joe had ripped his T-shirt but he was grinning like Puck. We ambled back into town then I walked Jane out to her house on the very edge of Shiplea. We squeezed hands at her front garden gate. I could hear the yowling and yahooing of a cowboy film coming from the television in her lounge. I didn't ask to come in to watch the sheriff get tomahawked and the squaws get lassoed. I wasn't invited in anyway.

All the way home I wasn't sure whether to float on clouds or trudge through quicksand.

In His seventh and final incarnation, God was an absence. We seek Him incessantly; wondering if He was ever actually there at all.

George Bloody Orwell

Confidential Memo
Originator: Colonel Peyton Farquar-Jones

Gentlemen,

Far be it from me to recognise any goodness in that rank socialist George Bloody Orwell, but his notion of rewriting the past as a means of exerting better control over the present has much to recommend it. And what a past I refer to! Did you know that the Ancient Egyptians had a creation myth in which the god Atum masturbates into his hand and then drinks the seminal fluid in order to fertilise it? Or that the Bantua people of the Congo River believe that their god Bumba vomited the world into being? We can't have crap like this shoved down our children's throats!

The Inner Council has decided, therefore, to stick with the Book of Genesis as it gives the right and proper male/female hierarchy as well as encouraging respect for an anthropomorphic creator. There are a few difficulties regarding absolute fundamentalism in the face of post-Renaissance scientific advances, but rest assured these will be ironed out. For the moment, it is imperative that we rid our glorious heritage of impure foreign mythologies and teach our citizens only what is right and true.

The Rise and Fall of the Universe

∞

In my parallel world my wife looks over my shoulder and asks, "Who's this hot Jane Wylie, then?"

And I say, "Oh, she's just someone I made up."

"Are you sure?" she continues.

And I add, "Well, she's based on someone I fancied at school. You know, first love and all that... It was all unconsummated, of course."

And she snorts, "Unconsummated, my arse!"

Then she traipses off to the kitchen to load up the cosmic dishwasher so I'll have another meaningful task to complete when I empty it at the end of the universe.

The Space Between the Asteroids

Astronaut Simon Cooper, Personal Log

Without over-judicious and illegal use of the Somnia machines, it is certain that the original crew of Nirvana One will die of old age before we reach any nearby stars or habitable planetary systems. Of course, the ship could run entirely automatically. We humans are just tinkering. However, whenever I close my eyes at rest break I feel sure I would know no comfort unless settling down with the knowledge that somebody was minding the shop.

The children and grandchildren of the frozen settlers will, of course, be educated to run and repair the ship as necessary. Much of their learning will consist of by then ancient Earth history and the social necessities for living peacefully together in an enclosed space. They will still find plenty of time to indulge in more artistic pursuits, not to say the characteristic courtship rituals and activities common to humankind since the days of the cave. To avoid the problem of inbreeding, our sperm banks contain a range of samples obtained from the Human Genome Project. Even those who didn't actually make it onto the ship may still send their children to the stars.

*

Transcript of interview broadcast via BBC television programme *Panorama* on 11th March

Newly elected Home Affairs Minister Peyton Farquar-Jones (PFJ) is questioned by journalist Gavin Meddler (GM)

GM: "Minister, let's talk a little about the Government's Intercourse Interdiction Bill, the so-called 'Sex Ban'. Are you confident of getting it through both Houses?"

PFJ: "Certainly. It's a clear, purposeful piece of legislation."

GM: "But only temporary?"

PFJ: "We hope so. We expect to bring the conjugal rights of married couples back on line within a year or so. Until then the Act will be all-inclusive."

GM: "With a lower age limit of eight?"

PFJ: "That's correct. This is to take account of differing rates of maturity amongst young girls. There is no upper age limit, by the way."

GM: "And what do you say to opponents who accuse you of meddling in the social habits, not to say God-given rights, of individual citizens?"

PFJ: "Firstly, one must always consider the greater good. Secondly, we have been accused of being too laissez faire. So now we are taking the strong moral lead which the electorate has been crying out for. Let me tell you, we have placed clear blue water between ourselves and the Moderate Alliance with their wishy-washy stance of 'A little bit of this is okay and a little bit of that but not too much'. In next year's election, if we hold one, the Alliance will pick up no more than a handful of votes. People want clear policies. Answers, direction, guidance, leadership – the British Normality Patrol offers all these and more."

GM: "But we're out of step with Europe on this."

PFJ (smiling): "We're often out of step with Europe. I prefer to see us as being one or two steps ahead. You mark my words, the world's problems are such that pretty soon most other civilised countries will be introducing something akin to the Intercourse Interdiction Act."

GM: "But it's completely unworkable. People will still have sex and you won't be able to stop them. Are you going to introduce compulsory daily medical checks for everyone over the age of consent?"

PFJ: "It's crossed our minds. But I think you've grabbed the wrong end of the stick, Gavin. We're asking citizens to look out for and look after their neighbours. Steer them away from temptation. It's the Christian thing to do."

GM: "It sounds like a perversion of Christianity to my ears. You just want to create a nation of snoops and peeping toms."

PFJ: "On the contrary, young man. Within – oh, a few months at most – there will be nothing worth snooping on or peeping at. Britain will be a place of moral rectitude again."

For a time, my affection for Jane Wylie was swamped and engulfed by small town boredom. There were all the family-run shops you'd been into a hundred times or more. For want of something else to do, you'd end up in Ross's buying fudge and coconut ice even though we'd all sworn off sweets for a week for the sake of our teeth and our flat white stomachs. It was the same with the funfair at Chesilham. Once you'd knocked your knees on the dodgems and grimaced into the convex mirrors one year, then you'd done it every year of your life.

I needed a harder kick.

It strikes me that exogamy is the most natural human impulse. Even though my outward search is sometimes more of a reaching inside.

From soft pursuits to macho stunts. From off the garden wall to bungee jumping. Air travel gives birth to space flight. You're happy sleeping with your wife but then after a while you lust for the woman across the street.

Maybe it's all some perverse death wish, a constant mantra:
"Faster, harder, more!
Faster, harder, more!"
We are daring death all the time by pushing at the limits of life. But then if you just sit still in the middle of the road where your mother abandoned you, pretty soon a juggernaut will come and run you over.

Is there a limit to human endeavour? Perhaps only if there is a limit to the space-time continuum. At some future date our hurrying and scurrying will mean that we catch up with the expansion wave of the Big Bang and start to push back the envelope, yelling, "Come on, get on with it!"

Important Public Notice

Lovely Ladies and Gallant Gentlemen of Albion's Isle! Your co-operation is politely requested.

Do you remember when Britain was truly Great? Do your parents or your grandparents? Once upon a time our Empire covered a quarter of the globe. We're not looking to reinstate imperialism. But not so long ago Britannia took a moral lead on the issues of the day and we believe she should do so again.

Medical evidence has proved conclusively that The Disease is sexually transmitted. Police files indicate that a high proportion of criminal activity is sexually motivated. Our own research shows that the simple enjoyment and pleasure in being alive, which is the birthright of all our citizens, is being polluted by a barrage of broadcasting and publishing of an overtly sexual nature.

And what is the common link here? Exactly! So it behoves us to proffer a solution. Initially, we intend to institute a voluntary code of conduct but legislation will follow if necessary. Therefore, we request that as from April 1st all British nationals, subjects and their dependants refrain from all forms of sexual activity. Similar rules will apply also to foreign visitors, immigrant workers and so forth. This is not a 'Sex Ban' as our detractors have labelled it; rather, we are advocating a period of voluntary celibacy.

Why is this necessary? Need you ask!

Just consider for a moment the mouth-watering prospect of a thriving, hard-working democracy where the back alleys have been cleared of drug pushers, rent boys and homeless urchins; where the gutters are clean enough to drink from rather than full of infectious spermatozoa and discarded condoms; where the wasted energy of the chase and the seduction is instead channelled into manufacturing prosperity and happiness for all. Imagine this country, Great Britain, competing again with the Germans, the Indians, the Yanks, the Chinese and the industrial nations of the Pacific Rim. It could happen, you know!

We are sure we can count on your support with this measure. The country will save millions on childcare, education, social security and the health service. The benefits to you personally could be immense. Why not work on that model boat you always intended to build? Remember the tapestry left half-completed two or three years ago? Why not take up a sport? When did England last have a World Champion or a Wimbledon winner? We could rectify the situation sooner than you think!

Don't forget, we've been elected to act in your best interests at all times but we need your co-operation, too.

Issued by the Central Government Think-Tank – "Even when it rains, our sun is shining!"

Dear Old Dutch Uncle Nicholas promises us that within twenty years humankind will have successfully invented a time machine. No doubt this is just another idle Sunday afternoon Science Club boast; but, if he's right, I don't want to visit famous wars or orgies, nor do I want to head on into the unknown Armageddon which probably lies ahead. Given the choice, I'd go backwards, right back as far as is conceivable, in order to answer the question: Where did the Big Bang start?

And I mean, specifically where. I've never been enamoured of this contention that everywhere is the centre and whichever way we look the universe is the same. If that's the case, maybe the heliocentrists are right and we are living right at the very middle of the cosmic maze and always have been. We should stop chasing the background radiation outwards and seek to return to its primal source.

Police Sergeant Robert Salt, Confidential Report Number XQ 2700
Since last year's State Security Act, we have had the budget and the manpower to investigate all claims and tip-offs taken by our branch office. The Heritage and Values Council has, in effect, handed us the task of eradicating all traces of British liberalism. The hell with 'Live and let live'! Such soppy and soft-headed

attitudes have seen this once great country sink into the second division of world powers. Wishy-washy talk of freedom of choice, self-fulfilment and respect for difference have historically left us in the position of still choosing a goalkeeper whilst the other team has kicked off and is on the attack. Ah, but now, it's no more grey areas! No more moral mazes and ethical dilemmas! Right is with us and it's a great time to be alive.

Opposition to the British Normality Patrol's restrictions has, of late, taken on a less overtly political form: pirate radio, spontaneous parties and concerts, fly-by-night shops selling so-called 'New Age' products... Given the hysteria and bunkum that was generated in my youth by the advent of the third millennium, it is no surprise to any of us that we have also experienced a rise in fortune telling booths and street peddlers proffering divination by tea leaves, Tarot cards and the heads and tails of the coins in your pocket. Technically, all these time-wasting activities are still within the letter of the law. Legislation has yet to catch up with these left field sidelines but the slightest suspicion sends us in, warrants in one hand, CS sprays and side-handle truncheons in the other.

We received a tip-off that the Seafront Fortune Telling Parlour owned by Monsieur and Madame Neptune of Belgravia was actually a front for sadomasochism and general brothel keeping activities. Two weeks of undercover investigation turned up nothing more salacious than a few palms crossed with silver. There were delectable young women around, to be sure, but they remained demure in dress and did not venture out unaccompanied after dark. The establishment seemed above board and beyond reproach. How could we hit them without evoking cries of unfairness and martyrdom?

We are nothing if not diligent. Since the creation of the EMPRESS unified computing system, every officer has had instant access to every piece of data and gossip relating to every living citizen, stretching back almost to the Dark Ages of card files and metal cabinets. We had a VAT query for Mr Neptune from half a decade ago. Not a crime or misdemeanour, just a query.

It was enough.

Where we'd hoped to find whips and manacles we found wholefood cookery books. Where we'd hoped to find syringes we found fishing tackle. Where we'd hoped to find mountains of pornography and pervy camcorder escapades we found a few '18' rated videos. The titles would have been considered acceptable adult viewing ten years ago but in these more responsible times such items have been de-certificated and should have been dumped in the amnesty bins twelve months ago. A fine and an injunctive closure of the premises would suffice for now.

The Prime Minister recently suggested, in a secret memo, that creativity and the puritan work ethic thrive with the sublimation of the sex drive. It is my belief that occasional fulfilment of the sexual impulse, even in these celibate times, is imperative to keep myself and my work force on our toes, so to speak. In my 'awaiting disposal' storeroom there is always a copious supply of lipsticks, lace, perfumes and aids to lovemaking. We are handsome, virile young men. What's more, we can offer the ultimate inducement: immunity from prosecution. I'm sure some of the lovely young palmists and crystal ball gazers will be more than willing...

Personal Log, Astronaut Simon Cooper

We have been absent from Earth for many months and yet have only lately reached the asteroid belt, that gravel strewn hazard of the space highway. The computers could cope unaided with this slalom navigation, of course, but at least the avoidance of these sharp boulders gives me a sense of purpose. Once these myriad fragments may have together formed a fifth rocky planet, a neighbour to rust red Mars and another potential harbour of life ahead of the uninhabitable gas giants. Pentavir, I once heard this conjectural world called.

My life aboard the star-bound Nirvana One has fallen into a strict routine of checks, reports, half-weight exercises and re-hydrated meals, All of this has become so much second nature that I have become almost as automatic as our life-supporting and life-transporting machines. Only my dreams and memories remain wilful and independent.

On balance, I am glad to be away from the morally stultifying atmosphere on Earth, even though this mission is the ultimate one-way ticket.

Earth Base assures us that our star colonising vehicle is the first of many but I have the suspicion that we represent the final throw of those particular dice. Technology has mostly stopped looking outwards and instead focused itself on the microscopic vortex of brain implants and bioengineering. Maybe it's because the Big Bang and the subsequently expanding universe really is too immense a concept for the human mind to adequately comprehend. We have tried to reach out but have generally only been able to stagger one or two short steps. The giant leap may of necessity prove to be an internal voyage.

Ricky Wells watched the helicopter swooping low over the nearby streets, its pencil of light an almost solid appendage cutting swathes through the gloom of early twilight. The beam was drawing criss-crossed spirals of photons like a psychopathic spirograph… and the end of all this webbed meandering would be to catch him because he'd been thinking obsessively about sex again. Shit, surely they couldn't really mind-read? He hadn't actually done anything, just pondered. His mate Bill reckoned the police had special ECG machines which could detect exactly what thoughts any given citizen was having – at a distance of up to half a mile! It was only natural that boys his age thought about wanking and shagging and feeling up young women. It was all to do with hormones. Best not to dwell on duplicitous nature, try to do something else...

The dopplering pulse of the chopper all but drowned out the TV programme he'd been watching. He ought to get on with his homework – bowdlerised research into the slave trade – but the box was always a friendly comfort in the corner, like a mobile he'd had above his cot when he was a baby. Even so, television wasn't what it used to be. No, really, he wasn't just holding the usual 'life is rubbish' teenage attitude; the ruling party's broadcasting restrictions meant that even ancient repeats suffered from ludicrous jump cuts as the lords and masters censored anything salacious or seditious.

The helicopter buzzed his street again. Its search beam flickered along the rowan trees outside Ricky's window. He recoiled, let the net curtain fall back into place, and began a panicky planning for a possible escape.

If only he hadn't started thinking about lovely Jane Whiteley when he was soaking in the bath last night. She was always demurely dressed but her eyes gave a hint of darker passion. Just enough for his brain and his hands to focus on. He'd cleared up afterwards and left the bathroom smelling pungently of Cif. His mother had wrinkled her nose, suspicious of his unusually good housekeeping. Maybe she'd shopped him! Or else his mate Bill was right and they really did filter all waste water to ascertain who had released spermatozoa into the sewage system.

This was once sunny, swinging London but Ricky was living in a climate of fear.

There was a wailing of sirens, a slamming of metal doors and a pounding of size thirteen boots as two white police vans screeched to a halt. At the top of his road! Heading onto the common next to the flats... not coming for Ricky, at least not for the moment. He could breathe and watch. A few inquisitive souls stepped out of their front doors to get a better vantage but, with the copter virtually hovering motionless over a clump of trees, Ricky had as good a view as any and, besides, he did not want to risk guilt by association.

Quite why it took ten officers to arrest one courting couple was a question only to be posed silently. The policemen dragged the bare-chested, bearded felon towards the first van and bundled him inside. His erstwhile girlfriend put up more of a struggle. She'd been caught *in flagrante* a hundred yards from her bed-sit. Subtlety and sexual desire were not always bedfellows. One of the constables had thrown a grey blanket over her shoulders but in the excitement she dislodged it and Ricky caught a groin swelling snapshot of her bare breasts, nipples and all. It was the most naked he'd seen a woman – live or image – in over two years.

The fornicatrix was unceremoniously bundled into the back of the second van. It did not occur to Ricky until an hour later that three policemen and no WPCs had accompanied the woman into the rear of the vehicle.

It was one of the cooler nights of the season. Simon wished he'd brought a scarf for his exposed ears. The sea breeze tried its disruptive best with his hair but it was too short and thinning to be much troubled by its tricks.

Here was Jane at last, with her requisite female accessories of blue sash and Virgin Mary headscarf in place. She almost walked past him. There was no public show of affection.

"Where are we going?" he asked.

"My dad's old beach hut. Where he used to watch the girls go by."

The tide line was gull-infested. The new moral codes had yet to crack the food litter problem. There were a few fishing boat lights on the horizon. Early starters or men keen to take a lengthy break from their families. The illicit couple stopped outside a nondescript door painted in flaky red. Jane jiggled the key nervously. Inside, there was a cupboard, a sink, a kettle, two chairs and a single bed with grey army blankets.

"I've run out of Marvel," she said.

"I'll take it black," he answered.

She pulled a two bar electric fire out from under the bed, plugged it into a socket near the door. Simon checked the curtains. Beyond them was the sea, crashing cacophonously on the shingles. Enclosed this side of the faded drapes was a shared space untouched by the ever stricter social conditions without.

"My mother's got the children," she volunteered.

"How long can you stay?"

"Don't ask. Some time… but not nearly enough."

The acrid coffee stung his tongue into momentary silence. They sat in the chairs, knees locked like a pair of iron gates, each waiting for the other to bridge the distance.

"Shall we... lie down and talk?" Simon ventured.

He kicked off his training shoes, squeezed up against the wall. His arm was under her thin body now and it was natural to seek her lips as she snuggled up next to him. His free hand squeezed her shoulder, moved down her arm and then up her white blouse, redeeming buttons, feeling inside to touch a tiny pointed nipple beneath her loose cotton bra. She struggled with his belt for a few seconds. He guided her fingers towards his zip. Foreplay was a luxury they had learned to live without.

The blankets were rough against their bare pink skin. Their love abided but their times together were snatched, fleeting, even desperate. This far and no further.

She dressed quickly afterwards. Even with the heater, it was cold in the hut. He wiped himself with some kitchen roll from his trouser pocket. He wished they could linger naked, undisturbed, unburdened...

"I must be going," she whispered.

"Stay a bit longer, Jane. Please."

She stroked his face. "Even this..."

He froze with a presentiment of danger. She looked anxiously from his eyes to the door. Nothing. Just the Moon-riled seas on the million year rocks. He smiled.

There was a loud knock at the door.

Neptune the Mystic

Neptune was a tuna fisherman whose prosperity in ancient times enabled him to live the lifestyle of a Greco-Roman god and, indeed, count Zeus among his kinsmen.

We picture him full-bearded, golden-crowned and armed with his trusty trident as the serpent-horses pull his gleaming chariot through the foam. Father of, and husband to, countless nereids he always knew where his next fornication was coming from.

Astronaut Simon Cooper, Personal Log

It is our intention to create a slingshot effect from the gravitational pull of Neptune. This is the only planet we shall be closely observing as we seek to leave our sun's influence forever.

The eccentric orbit of Pluto has for some decades caused the ultramarine Neptune to be the outermost major body in the solar system, but things are reverting to normal now. The deep blue gas giant presents a doleful face, its rings barely visible; the eye is pulled, however, by the Great Dark Spot of its weather system which gives this side of the orb the appearance of an unutterably sad visage.

    We believe that, in keeping with its mythical
nomenclature, the royal blue hydrogen atmosphere shields
a hidden ocean composed of warm water and gases.
    Would that we could dive deep down into its
welcoming waves and swim with beautiful nereids.

He lost her somewhere in the Haunted House. More of a van, really, an open-sided pantechnicon which was dark and full of fake cobwebs but otherwise relied on the punter to concoct his own unlit nightmares.

Now she was several stalls away, sticking darts into already perforated playing cards. Last night's prize coconut had proved mouldy when she'd cracked it open but liquorice allsorts kept quite well even with travelling funfairs.

He hoped to catch her in the Hall of Mirrors but the grotesqueries and fractures were just the usual illusions dealt to the unwary and inquisitive alike. By an effort of will and a crossing of palms with silver, Simon was able to share a carriage with Jane on the Waltzer and the aerial ellipse of the Paratrooper, but in both cases centrifugal force served to force their bodies apart somewhat.

Miss Neptunia the Fortune Teller dealt him five Tarot cards. The last one was Death, which was not to be interpreted literally or immediately but rather as the necessity of breaking past bonds and seeking new horizons.

When the generator for the dodgem track fizzled, sputtered and burnt out like a miniature supernova, it was clearly time to go home to a warm single bed back at his mother's house.

Continued Debriefing of Simon Cooper – temporary flight commander of United Earth starship 'Nirvana One' – by General Oliver de Montford, Earth Base

SIMON: When John Couch Adams and Urbain Le Verrier discovered Neptune it was a mere point of light. Seen in close up, however, the ultramarine orb resembled more and more a doleful face, with its huge down-turned blue-black spot reminding us all of a sombre mouth. Despite the romance and excitement of space travel, which never diminishes, most of the time we decided to blank out the view screen and its sorrowful picture during our approach towards the eighth planet.

GENERAL: Why, exactly?

SIMON: The huge sphere was like a giant mirror to our own depressed, lonely mood... That was to change, of course.

GENERAL: When did you first become aware of the extra-terrestrial presence?

SIMON: They appeared initially as a vaporous cloud where none should be. They encircled the ship, kept pace with us... it was like travelling through permanent mist. It reminded me of a sea fog from my childhood days in Shiplea. Indeed, the initial effect of the cumular apparition was to make us all thoughtful and nostalgic for everything we'd left behind on Earth. Eddie called a crew meeting at which all the relays, cameras and microphones that beamed our every waking moment back to home base were temporarily blocked or shut down. No doubt this caused consternation back at Mission Control, but we needed the privacy which several thousand million kilometres should have given us automatically as a right. The overwhelming feeling was that we should abandon the mission. Even those who wanted to press on were only keen to do so in order to gain incontrovertible evidence that the solar system was closed and that a hundred years or more of astronomical research had led to a frightening accumulation of completely illusory data caused by the reflections from the barrier.

GENERAL: Yes, but when did the sex vampires appear?

SIMON: They weren't vampires, although maybe, to use an old Hollywood term, some of them were vamps! We gradually became aware of their presence on board ship over the next few hours. We had grown used to the strange creakings and settlings of the plastics and metals of our craft. At first, it was believed that the computer had prematurely revived some of the colonists. This was an idea which had passed through one or two of our late night unrecorded conversations. Indeed, I had caught Wild Jack gazing lovingly at the doe-like face of a sleeping xeno-biologist, with his fingers poised above the resuscitation buttons and – it seems really twee, but it's true – his lips unconsciously mouthing the words to the song *If You Were the Only Girl in the World*!

GENERAL: What was the initial reaction to the appearance of the creatures?

SIMON: Suspicion, naturally. A feeling of mass hallucination. Then, as these at first rather homogenous women began to take on more individual characteristics, an overwhelming feeling of extraordinary desire.

GENERAL: I see. Even if the fulfilment or attempted fulfilment of this desire would jeopardise the safety of yourself and your fellow crew members and would contravene several Class One regulations regarding United Earth Space Administration conduct?

SIMON: I couldn't help it. She became everything I ever wanted in my life.

Astronaut Simon Cooper, Personal Log

And all the way out, that ghostly music came piping over the ship's intercom: dour duh, dour duh, doo, dee dour... as if it was an incantation calling up the spirits of the ether, the lonely siren call of space, discovered and notated in a form more popularly accessible than, and in any case predating, the digital chatter of the radio telescope. Had Gustav Holst known that the wraiths waited around the orbit of Neptune? Was he an emissary, a messenger rather than a mere human being with a talent for bird-track marks on five bar gates?

Those ethereal female voices – "Aah-aah, aah-aah-aah" – no words, just archetypal vibrations of the larynx. Heard so often, become so internalised that we would have been surprised not to encounter the original source of the hypnotic call.

Debriefing Continues

GENERAL: Just what did these wraiths offer which was so attractive to you?

SIMON: In a word, sex, I suppose. All manner of forms or positions. We were lonely men up there. We'd come from an Earth under the injunction of the Intercourse Interdiction Act. We were following our natural impulses. What else were we to do?

GENERAL (scoffing): Natural impulses? These creatures weren't even human! Did you not consider the dangers?

SIMON: We all considered the dangers – to varying degrees. Some held back much longer than others. The nereids allowed us to carry out several biological tests which assured us that we were not at risk from the conventional Earthly dangers of accidental impregnation and the spread of infection. Put yourself in my place: If the old-fashioned theories of an expanding universe were to prove true, I would never make landfall again. Part of the time I actually wondered whether I'd already died and had woken up surrounded by angels. It was a male chauvinist caveman fantasy. The wraiths were beautiful, compliant, intelligent company, also; but without ever making us feel small. It is my only desire to explore the outer reaches of Neptune again... But I won't manage it this side of the big sleep.

*

Astronaut Simon Cooper, Personal Log

Soon no one on board the 'Nirvana' was seen without their accompanying space nereid. We were not prevented by their presence from fulfilling the necessary daily chores on board ship. Everything felt so right with our wraiths beside us. It was as if the old Greek philosophy had finally come true and we had found our other halves.

Admittedly, our attention was not always wholly on the furtherance of the mission. No sleepers were put in jeopardy but otherwise we largely ignored the angry screeches from Mission Control back on fundamentalist Earth. The 'Nirvana' became something of a sex haven as we discarded the baggage of inhibitions we had carried out here with us.

At first my angel took on the physical form of Jane Wylie, the originally listed captain of the mission and the woman I had chased through the sea, the sand and the centuries. Jane had fallen pregnant – by her husband – a few weeks before blast–off. Although it was within the bounds of legal matrimony, they'd clearly broken the Intercourse Interdiction Act. However, a smart lawyer cited a loophole that they'd both been on compassionate time at the British base in Tenerife, not necessarily under the homeland jurisdiction. Whatever, it had seemed better all round that she cement over the cracks in her marriage and remain Earthbound.

I missed her desperately. Even the vastness and eternal beauty of deepening space had so far failed to comfort me. I knew the angel was not really Jane even though she possessed her look and several of her mannerisms.

After a time, however, my visitor's form became fuller, rounder, fairer of hair, scent still female but a little less acidic. Her skin seemed softer still, her full breasts a pillow to my erstwhile loneliness, her supple feet curling with my caresses and then wrapped over my shoulders as I entered her yet again.

"It's still me, Simon," she whispered, "but I'm more my own person now. I've looked into your mind to discover what is desire and what is simply memory."

I noticed also differences in the other companions as I reconnoitred the ship: subtle shifts in skin tone, hair colour, height, disposition.

"Don't call me Jane, any more," she whispered. "Make it Miranda. I'm sure that's mythical and spatial enough for you," she added with a girlish grin.

The latest squawking from Earth spoke of evolutionary dead ends and vampiric parasitism.

Even if it was all revealed as possession, or indeed illusion, I had to admit that I had never been so contented.

Debriefing Continues

SIMON: They made us question our future. We were never able to undeniably ascertain whether they worked through physical or merely cerebral stimulation. Certainly the angels had a physical presence and this is borne out by their variously vague to full registration on photographic film. They made us question so many of our assumptions. Is the point of evolution to improve or to transcend the body? Should we be looking to become floating entities like the space nereids? And, even if we are presently limited to an existence within a closed solar system, is it not the case that all walls visible from within possess also an outside?

*

Debriefing Continues

GENERAL: Tell us again, Mr Cooper, why you signed up for this particular mission?

SIMON: I was in love with Jane Wylie. I was dogging her footsteps, following her career path, trying desperately to keep up with her shooting star success. It was the ultimate Adam and Eve dream – she and I founding a new world.

GENERAL: But you would both have been dead by landfall.

SIMON: Well, our children, then.

GENERAL: But she was already married when you developed this infatuation.

SIMON: Yes... and that was to be her downfall. Three months pregnant, she was suddenly barred from leading the mission. Facing a damaging court case, too. At that point the crew was evenly balanced, male and female, and a range of relationships seemed eminently probable. The unfortunate test accident and the exceptionally high scores of the back-up crew led to an all-male enclave.

GENERAL: And when this space vampire metamorphosed into human female form it was feeding on both on-board computer data banks and, telepathically, your thoughts and memories. Am I correct?

SIMON: Yes.

GENERAL: So that this blood-drinking, mind-eating, sperm-sucking parasite could present itself in a form highly desirable?

SIMON: Yes. The wraiths made it easy for us to fall in love with them. We were like the sailors with Ulysses falling for the sirens, I know. It all sounds so stupid and penile in the cold light of an Earth day but they emanated also this incredible sense of goodness. They were personal angels, not parasites.

Debriefing Continues

GENERAL: Why did you terminate the mission?

SIMON: We had no choice. There was nowhere to go.

GENERAL (irritably): Your sworn duty was to continue piloting the ship beyond the boundaries of the solar system and to seek to establish a human colony around a nearby star.

SIMON: There is nothing beyond the solar system; at least nothing we can get to.

GENERAL: You aborted the mission at Neptune. You didn't even push on to Pluto!

SIMON: But the angels, or wraiths or 'sex vampires' as you call them, took us out to the edge. They showed us where the limit of our sphere is. Every piece of data which has been apparently received and interpreted back on Earth for a hundred, a hundred and fifty years... it's all false signals and reflections – not quasars and pulsars and spiral galaxies... This barrier, this wall, it's not a solid wall, it's more like an absorbent sludge of indefinite consistency. But it's there.

GENERAL: The barrier is a simple hallucination. You were drained of vital bodily fluids, drugged by your despicable escapades with these alien beings, then sent back in disgrace.

SIMON: It was no hallucination, General. Check through the data banks of the Stellavistic Guidance Computer. Everything I've told you, apart from the intensity of the experience, which of course is a personal matter, everything I've told you is completely objective.

*

Simon and Miranda had started to make love down on the cargo deck where the porthole windows offered a backdrop of pincushion stars or the deep blue countenance of Old Father Neptune. Who needed the Moon for romance nowadays? Besides which, the false gravitation was a little stronger here and sex was more like the old-fashioned Earth variety. Not that Miranda knew first-hand about such things.

She'd complained of dizziness and fatigue. Their bodies disengaged. Simon offered her free run of the First Aid cabinets.

"It's nothing, I'll be okay," she muttered.

Clothing had largely been dispensed with aboard the 'Nirvana One'. Simon had helped the space nereid back to his cabin. They passed no one on the way. In the soft light – in any light, and even without light, with just touch, taste and smell – it was hard to believe she wasn't really a woman born from sperm and egg.

"Come and join me, Simon," she insisted.

"Are you sure?"

"It's what I want more than anything."

He smiled. "I'll just fix a drink first. Do you want one?"

"Whatever you're having."

The recent change in the angels' natures to enable the imbibing of refreshments as well as the recreational juices of saliva and, yes, semen had made the women seem more Earthly than ever. No doubt medical scanners could still tell a tale, but appearance and action were wholly convincing.

"Simon, I'm getting lonely..."

"What's a few more seconds after a two million year wait?" he asked.

"And what's that supposed to mean?"

"Nothing. Just being playful."

His right hand caressed her bare buttocks. The skin was smoother than glass, but more mysterious than a newly discovered crystal. He entered her from behind, her pear-shaped cheeks ruffling his tightly curled pubes. He moved gently but rhythmically, arcing away from her except where they were conjoined, his body forming a rough crescent as his blood stiffened penis sought to make up for all the years of rejection and under-nourishment.

After orgasm he dozed briefly, no more than thirty seconds. When he opened his eyes again Miranda had disappeared. Somehow he knew immediately that she wasn't simply taking a toilet break or conjuring up a coffee. He screamed her name. Once, twice, a dozen larynx curdling times. He hadn't cried since boyhood but now he was inconsolable, yang parted from yin.

Instinctively, he knew she had gone forever. No warning, no evidence apart from the microscopic skin cells which would wash off him the moment he stood under the shower. Even within her arrival she'd somehow conveyed the inevitability of her departure. Had she absorbed enough of his life force for now, feeding on lust, passion and sticky milk from his penis? Or else had he somehow used up hers, dug so deep that she had no more love or energy to impart and had simply vanished into the ether?

Dressed, but still unwashed, Simon made a tour of the ship. The place was like the overdose clinic of a space-borne casualty ward. The all-male crew was stumbling around as if released from enchantment or woken suddenly from the deepest of dreams. After one hundred years the pots started boiling again in Briar Rose's castle... Except in this instance the monitors and life-support systems had functioned with perfect normality all along. Combined wish fulfilment? A deception caused by the ripples in the barrier at the solar system's edge? Or a real-life drama brought to sudden, awful truncation?

There was a message on its way from Earth Base. The last several had been deliberately ignored, a churlish act which maybe impinged in some way upon their present predicament. Everyone – every Earthling; yes it was now merely every man for himself – was gathered in the control lounge. Simon felt he detected the traitorous scent of snake amongst his colleagues. But who?

The Colonel's familiar visage bloomed onto the view screen.

"Gentlemen," he began, "your troubles are over. Thanks to your continued posting of data we have had our scientists working around the clock to chemically analyse the nature of the sex vampires – "

There were shouts of disagreement, catcalls which were not transmitted but somehow expected as the Colonel's talking head paused momentarily. Simon noticed that Eddie didn't join in the furore. Was he to blame?

"We have," the Colonel continued, "at great expense, directed an experimental particle beam at your craft which, if successful, will eradicate the evil parasites but leave you and the sleeping colonists unharmed. If you are receiving this, then you will feel thankful that we have toiled so hard to secure your release. If you are not receiving this, then I and my staff have egg on our faces and a court martial on our tails."

There was another pause but this time no one spoke. In a dramatic sotto voce – 2,700 million miles distant and he still couldn't resist a theatrical flourish – the Colonel added, "You are to continue with the mission. That is the explicit instruction from the Ruling Council. It was a majority verdict rather than unanimous. If I had my way I'd jump into a rocket right now and come out and castrate the frigging lot of you. But orders are orders..."

Philip blanked the screen. "I don't believe it, any of it," he muttered.

"Then where are the angels?" asked Jack.

"I don't know. All I've got is questions, fucking piles of them with no sign of any sense-making answers. Leave me alone!"

"Looks like we're all gonna be alone for a long, long time," Eddie commented.

Simon gave him a lengthy stare. "Let's give it... four hours and meet back here. Think things over. Plan for the future."

"We know the future," interrupted Jack. "They want us to go on with the mission."

"That's their future," Simon replied, "which is not necessarily ours. They've taken away the thing that made my life worth living and frankly I'm in the mood to nuke Earth Base and the whole fucking planet. We could turn this craft around and go back as a nuclear bomb. Oh, hell, I want to think it all through for a while. Agreed?"

A few nods and mumbles.

"I just wish Helen was still with me," Philip said.

"And Miranda."

"And Carlita."

"Rosemary."

"Guinevere."

"Jane Wylie."

Debriefing Continues

GENERAL (angrily): Quite apart from the staggering cost of this aborted star trip, what I really cannot stomach is your overweening arrogance. The sheer hedonism of your actions appals me! Were we not a civilised society, I would have you unceremoniously executed.

SIMON: The only reason you keep me and the others alive is because deep down you know we're telling the truth.

GENERAL: Truth? Lies? What do you know? Most of your life is merely a wet dream – at the taxpayer's expense! How do you think we felt being subjected to your pornographic home videos when what we expected and what we'd paid for was hard data on the nature of the universe?

SIMON: It wasn't pornography, it was the most beautiful experience of my life... And, anyway, you shouldn't have been watching.

Ex-Astronaut Simon Cooper, Personal Log

Several months have now passed since my inglorious return and my life, and that of my erstwhile colleagues, has settled into a predictable but comfortable routine. I live quietly on a largely unspoilt stretch of coastline just a few miles from the town of my birth. Despite our deliberate abortion of the mission the powers at Earth Base have dealt very fairly with us and absolved us from much of the blame. I am still in touch with several significant figures from my time as a space explorer but for much of the day I am completely alone with the beach, the waves, my thoughts and my memories.

I have fallen into the seemingly unavoidable cliché trap of all seasoned travellers in that I have returned from my voyage into space with the urgent need to secure the future of my starting point: Earth. Apart from the occasional unmanned satellite launched into perilous orbit around the home sphere, the space programme has been completely wound down. Effectively, I have been pensioned off.

For what they are worth, I have published my memoirs. They are full of cod philosophy and subjective impressions for which I often make effusive apology and yet my own limited viewpoint is the only window open to me. Of course!

The universe is a giant reflection and extension of everything we've ever done, thought or dreamed. Its paradigm is there in every volcano; every bleached, spiny, blindly swimming mollusc; in the molecules of the blood and the blue flames of burning methane. Our world is a fragile electron spinning round its neutron star.

Doubtless my rather muffled existence blinds me to the enormous suffering still endured by millions of Earth's inhabitants, but it seems to me that we have entered a golden millennium, finally getting to grips with a whole gamut of environmental and social problems which we allowed to almost engulf us during the careless centuries prior to now.

I have become completely trusting of our glorious leaders – I must be losing my mind!

The combined effects of partial use of the Somnia machines and low-level Einsteinian relativity mean that I have aged less than my Earthbound contemporaries. Absent from the technological advances intrinsic to a continuously developing society, I am at one and the same time an astronaut and a barbarian. Those I loved and was close to before my departure are now my spurious elders. I portray myself as part of a generation in limbo. It's just another handy excuse to classify myself as 'spaceman–philosopher–caveman'.

Some computer whiz kid has even turned our experiences with the nereids whilst orbiting Neptune into a cerebral simulation. The simulation is involving and convincing but not wholly so. Earth morality has relaxed recently. Many things are now permissible as long as they only take place inside the brain.

Jane Wylie, old before my time, is lost to me. The unimaginable reaches of deep space are lost to me, also. Miranda waits somewhere around the ultramarine planet. The days trickle by in contemplation and with a degree of contentment.

All explorations begin with an idea. Some go no further.

Light into Darkness?

Personal Log of Simon Cooper, Ex-Astronaut

Final conjecture:

From the mind of a nutter locked in his lonely garret:

Everything in the universe is patterned on the totality. The brain of Homo sapiens, is greater than your common or garden Neanderthal and is due to expand dramatically, not to say artificially, during the new millennium. Clearly, this brain with its points of light and its strung-out matter and its wide empty spaces is a microcosmic model of the cosmos.

Looked at another way, the entire universe is one unimaginably gigantic mind whose thought processes we merely glimpse as un-cracked codes from the superheated stars.

Such immensity is too much to comprehend and of necessity we limit our vision to this country, this world, our Luna neighbour... this moment, this hour, this century of being.

90% of the matter in the universe is still unexplained even in our narrow, humanistic (usually wrong) way. This so-called 'dark matter' is incomprehensible but necessary, invisible but omnipresent. In fact, were I looking for a final revelation, I would say it contains all the required ingredients.

Faith has long since deserted me and all I'm doing is playing with words and concepts but, with nothing else left to cling to, I throw this final hypothesis into the mix:

The dark matter is God.

Additional Chapters

Cosmic Scrapbook

Jupiter's Great Red Spot

Depending upon your perspective, Jupiter is either a successful giant planet or a failed 'not quite massive enough' star. More than three hundred times bigger than our paltry Earth, the banded planet revolves at an astonishing rate: clocking in with a sub-ten hour day.

Its Great Red Spot is thought to be an enormous cyclone in the upper atmosphere, so pigmented due to the upward suction of phosphorus. Siding with a left-handed universe, this high-pressure system rotates in an anti-clockwise direction. The facial feature was first spotted in 1660 by the British astronomer Robert Hooke. One is tempted to believe this supra-terran pimple is the result of Jove's wick-dipping past when no maiden fair or foul was safe from his kingly attentions. Spectroscopic analysis shows that Jupiter is mostly composed of hydrogen, confirming earlier suspicions that Jove's declarations of desire and fidelity were really so much hot air.

Bodily Mass

When I was four years old, I wouldn't venture out of the house during rain showers for fear of being knocked unconscious by plummeting canines and felines.

Much later I was fascinated by the street hoarding claims – "Ladies – Lose TEN POUNDS of unwanted fat in just two weeks". My mother shook her head and muttered something paradoxical about no such thing as free lunches but my imagination began to run wild. The adverts themselves – for competing diets, lotions, clinical treatments and so forth – proliferated like a plague. Svelte champion slimmers were regularly seen on local bulletins and even children's news roundups.

I remained puzzled. Where did all this superfluous stodge go? Dutch Uncle Nicholas, a since disgraced one-time family friend, regularly insisted that the amount of matter in the universe remains constant and, short of synthesis of suitable antimatter, could not actually be destroyed.

His explanations were in fact less wordy and more suited to my developing mind, of course; the accompanying hand gestures were, however, deemed unacceptable.

It seemed clear to me that, what with gravity, magnetism and all that jazz, the whole glutinous mass of discarded globules would congregate either in clumps like oily asteroids or in some sort of greasy ring at the edge of our solar system. I was concerned that the more corpulence we let go, the more confined we were by an oleaginous barrier just beyond the orbit of Pluto. One day we might be completely enclosed within this greasy bubble, suffocated like insects in amber.

Adulthood has taught me differently. No matter that I walk to work and take regular exercise and do not spend every evening slumped in front of a TV or PC, I find my midriff widening and the stick limbs of youth turning inevitably to plumped-pillow roundness.

All those unwanted pounds of flesh rejected by all those thousands upon thousands of slimmers were not displaced spatially, but simply *in time*. Now they are returning with a vengeance.

First Movement

Music has claims to be both the common language and indeed the very nature of the universe.

Let's briefly adopt a religious standpoint, for the sake of elucidating a sad point regarding our futile existence.

The one we know as the Creator might be more correctly described as the Composer, setting the whole symphonic suite in motion and achieving radical counterpoints and degrees of textural harmony beyond human understanding. Manuscript in hand and trusting his magnum opus to no one else, he becomes also the cosmic conductor. Here in our far-flung corner of the orchestra pit we struggle to interpret or even recognise his directions. It matters little: in the greater scheme of things we are largely unheard.

Gravity

Reputedly discovered by Sir Isaac Newton back in the 1660s when an apple fell on his head. It seems unlikely that this was the very same fruit involved in the much earlier Fall of Man, as Eve's playfulness is solemnly termed. Nor would it be the self-same apple split by the Swiss hero William Tell's accurate arrow.

Gravity is in many ways the ultimate pulling power. Newton also allegedly invented the cat-flap, which works on a simple pushing motion, so he was adept in either direction. Today's physicists are in search of a 'Theory of Everything'. Gravity is the force that just won't fit, but there's no getting away from it.

Second Movement

The music of the spheres is all very well but even the most entrancing elegies come to an eventual end. Maybe we'll be lucky enough to reach a repeat mark which will require us to play the last four billion bars all over again. Or maybe the whole of human civilisation is a mere dot behind a crotchet and we'd better make the most of it because it's time to move on to the next note which doesn't include our existence.

Possibly the piece goes like this: Silence – always everything begins thus; The Big Bang – a clash of timpani, a cymbal wave reverberating endlessly in all directions; and to follow… who knows? We are still within the compass of that first percussive strike.

How will it feel when the strings and woodwind come in?

Solsville

Once all the rage amongst excitement-minded immortals, many of the universe's theme parks and planetary playgrounds have lately fallen into a sad state of disrepair and under-use. Though paling in comparison with such state of the art amusement complexes as Orion's blue event horizon and the endless micro-chromatics of the Andromedan dust spiral, Solsville is still worth a look every few billion years or so.

The first ride, the cold and barren Pluto, is rather unprepossessing and even the recent addition of a closely orbiting satellite has failed to produce the gravitational shenanigans we Burst take such delight in experiencing. Simply, when you've rolled the rim of a black hole these two icy balls of rock aren't going to do much for you.

Things pick up somewhat with the blue gas giants of Uranus and Neptune but it is the multi-ringed Saturn which remains a major attraction for most visitors. Be prepared for some major league queuing if you want to try your hand at speed skating in either direction.

Jupiter provides a range of refuelling stations, as you might expect from such a large sphere of bilious hydrogen. Eating is strictly *al fresco*. Some find its phosphorus storms and cloud bands rather too bracing; if so, try one of the smaller franchises on Io or Callisto.

Younger Burst are generally much taken with the stone-stepping possibilities of the asteroid belt, which was once a paradisial place called Pentavir. Those of you with a highly developed historical turn of mind might like to explore the Martian relics of our late lamented brother species, the Burroughvians. The red planet itself is a partially restored monument to their artistry and architecture. Quietude and contemplation are required as the essential keys to unlocking the extant memories of their canals, pyramids and beautiful death culture. Russet dust has obscured many of their finest achievements. Engage your deep sensors for the full experience.

It is on the two innermost planets that the lack of funding for upgrading and redevelopment is most apparent. Mercury has slipped too close to Sol and offers nothing except very long days, equally long nights and a rather monochrome twilight zone. In earlier ages, Venus was a fecund playground devoted to proliferation and procreation of all sorts. Its sensual jungle remains now a mere memory amidst the heat, the wind and the sulphur.

The third planet, the pedestrianly named Earth, provides possibly the most exciting ride on offer to jaded space travellers. Still mostly blue and white from a distance, its increasingly carbonated atmosphere is a-buzz with primitive but still tingly wave transmissions whose cumulative effect is pleasantly narcotic. This is the only place in the solar system currently populated by indigenous life forms. The dominant species is a hairless simian whose overt aggression is matched only by its overwhelming sexual proclivities. Incredibly, these humans have somehow stumbled upon weaponry potentially fatal to the otherwise immortal Burst. That they have not yet successfully harnessed this capability is down to an ongoing programme of force-fed misinformation by our Higher Council.

Nevertheless, Earth is worth a visit if only for that necessary theme park frisson of possible danger at every twist and turn.

Binary Stars

This is the nature of my love for you.

I will stay close by you for my whole life.

Nothing can come between us and nothing can tear us apart.

If we produce children we shall rear them with equal affection and diligence.

Though one of us might be said to be the junior partner, yet we are both flaming giants locked into a torrid love affair which only aeons of time and our ultimate death and decay can ever bring to an end.

You shine for me and I am bathed in your glory. I blaze for you and you are washed with my brilliance.

We hold together and grow old together.

Let them proclaim the great marriages of yore: Romeo and Juliet, Isis and Osiris, Rama and Sita. Ours endures when theirs are mere dust and memory.

Let them not speak of us in solitary terms but always as one indivisible couple.

I will gaze upon you all my days and shall not ever think of our mutual attraction as entrapment.

Music From the Spheres

Introduction by Festival director Sylvia Simonsen:

Welcome to the programme accompanying tonight's premier performance of Arthur Holkham's lost opus: *Music from the Spheres*. This promises to be a unique, life-changing event and it is fitting that, given the demanding nature of what you are about to hear and be exposed to, I should offer a few explanatory words and background details.

Of Arthur himself, there is not much to tell. He was a secondary school science teacher for several unhappy years, struggling to impart facts and theories to recalcitrant teenagers. After retiring, he turned his passions for astronomy and music composition into an indoor hobby to occupy the rain-swept and windy days. When the clouds cleared, he could be found upon the Norfolk beaches with his trusty metal detector.

There is some mystery about his early personal life. He may have married – the relevant parish records were destroyed in a church fire. If he did wed, his wife must have also perished quite early – during Holkham's later years, he seemingly never had a close partner, either female or male. His contribution to education was negligible. Likewise, he would be forgotten to both science and music were it not for the diligent estate keeping of one of his latter day pupils, Simon Cooper. Mr Cooper discovered several extant copies of Holkham's self-published works, printed under the moniker with which his students lumbered him. Titles such as *The Hocus Pocus Guide to the Solar System* and *Hocus Pocus Rock Pool Lore* offered little beyond the quaint ruminations of a curious English eccentric. But there was more. Much more.

Through his magnum opus, the suite with the pencilled title *Music from the Spheres*, Holkham offers a work that seeks to create a link between quantum physics, the Big Bang, religion and orchestral composition. If genuinely original to this one odd old geezer, the cosmology and musical creativity is quite astonishing. Talk about lights hidden under bushels.

Arthur's Diary

Bloody children making so much sodding noise! Don't they teach them to sit still and read these days?

"Hey, give it a rest out there, you hooligans!"

"Fark off you ol' ponce!"

It will be half an hour at least before they tire of their tinny mobile phone ring tones and the kicking of stones and tree branches. Maybe even three-quarters of an hour. What was that experiment they were trying at the London tube stations and in some of the shopping malls? Playing classical music to bore and disperse the youths. But that was proper classical music – Beethoven, Mahler, Bach and Mozart – not the advanced material I am hoping to work on. Besides, if I put on one of the old symphonies now it would break my contemplation even worse than having delinquents in the front yard and I will end up borrowing; imitating rather than innovating. No, I shall have to play the waiting game.

Info datum deposited by XZ– 43/A:
As the scientists of the so-called twenty–first century were to the caveman, so we star travellers are to them. And yet we hold fast to some of the ideas that difficult era spawned. None more so than the theory of The Burst. These were the first beings to inhabit the universe, arriving fully formed pretty soon after, or even *within*, the first three minutes of the Big Bang. No one has yet conquered the cosmos in quite the same way as these originals but we are certainly trying. The Blink Drive has made us masters of space with the old physical and, let's be honest, psychological wall of the speed of light now surmounted like a mere molehill in a garden. And all thanks to the theorising and composition of one of the late twentieth / early twenty–first century's outside thinkers, Arthur Holkham. Almost all the great thinkers are outside thinkers, at least in their prime. Sometimes – like with Einstein or Newton – their ideas are embraced within their lifetime but often it takes death and temporal distance to allow the wine of original thought to mature and seep into the common pool. So it has been with the Hocus Pocus musical oeuvre and the astrophysical theories that accompanied them.

Temporal distance. Yes, that is the key quest for the *unforeseeable* future. To travel so fast and far that we are actually going back, heading always towards that mythical centre, that starting point. The Burst left us mere genetic memories of their existence and every hymn or fable we have concocted since is a warped version of their memory. We can progress so much faster than light. The challenge is to travel so fast that we roll back the years, the billions of years, and make contact with these first beings, these true supra-normal progenitors.

```
And when we meet, what will we ask?
    Or will we abase ourselves and decide that in
the endless quest of human curiosity, we have perhaps
pushed too far?
    Bring it on, boys.
```

Arthur's Diary

I like to think that my most creative moods occur when there is only the gentle, rhythmic rise and fall of the tide to keep me company through the insomniac nights. What they call background white noise – my heartbeat, the ticking of a clock, the occasional bird cry and the soft water tickling the hard shingles. All ignorable or able to be assimilated without distraction. The reason why poets used to locate to remote villas by a lake – to get away from it all.

And yet, going back over my composition, it seems that I am most inspired when I am battling against the tearaways and their moped racing or drunken phone calls right outside my window. Maybe my fire is up on these occasions and my focus is firmer for the challenge.

The Burst, of course, faced no such problems. The universe was so new and they were so fully formed, these original and originating super-beings, that they set their own rules. And also the pattern for their future which is now our present... and future, too.

I was brought up to go to Sunday school and to draw pictures of Jesus and Mary but the miracles of science soon superseded and obliterated those of burning bushes and loaves and fishes in my consciousness. I threw biblical creationism out on the junk heap of human ideas. Blazing like a nova, I was full of fiery ideas as a young student; these were mostly laughed off or, more politely, considered as mere science fiction plot devices, by my fusty old tutors. So I quietened, retreating into an intellectual shell. Now I am the fusty old man... but the fiery ideas still blaze.

There was no God or Creator starting the ball of Earth rolling. Nor was there a supernatural presence behind – or ahead of! – the Big

Bang. But the cosmos has not always been how it is now. When new, everything was vibrant, exciting, novel. The true creativity flourished in those first moments, minutes and years (excuse the human terms, I have nothing else to use) closely succeeding that incident we label the Big Bang. Everything was up for grabs then and the very matter of the macrocosm was more malleable. And The Burst were creative beings, full of ideas and plans. They had to be: there was nothing much around them, it required their making.

A philosopher once said that the highest of the arts is music and that all other forms – painting, poetry, whatever – aspire to the condition of music. The Burst knew this instinctively. They were the original composers. Noodling at first, trying out a glissando here and a chord progression there, but soon masters of their profession.

This is my big idea, the great Arthur Holkham theory, the contention that I wish to go public with... but will doubtless be dismissed just like I have always been dismissed. Perhaps posterity will uncover and disseminate it like the paintings of van Gogh or the stories of Franz Kafka. Maybe somebody else, somebody more photogenic and respected by the vacuous public, will come to the same or similar conclusion and take the credit and kudos. So be it.

The Burst were musicians. The galaxies were their tools and instruments. We are living inside an almost unimaginably gigantic composition. The whole history of the universe is an unfolding symphony played out on the cosmic scale. The stars, the planets, the nebulae are all components of this ongoing score.

Of course, we don't actually hear it in the conventional sense. There is no air in space to make the percussive waves to please or entice the human ear. The notes, if one can call them that, are in an entirely different register way beyond our consciousness and understanding. The harmonics would mash our brains were they not so dissipated by grand distances and a tempo designed for a performance that has already lasted more than thirteen billion years rather than Mozart's or Beethoven's more conventional twenty-five to forty minutes. Even Wagner would be a mere hiccough against the fabulous orchestration set in motion by The Burst. The forces we recognise, the forces we theorise, are all components in the playing out of this mighty operatic production. Gravity, magnetism, heat exchange – it's all part of the show, boys and girls. Determinism mostly wins the day because every atom of matter is playing its part as required by the original manuscript. Each sun registers on a musical scale beyond our comprehension. The music is not simply aural – you must get over that limitation. But it is music nonetheless. Written by the very first beings. Our puny planet resonates in harmony with the rest of the universe. And for all our ruination of this fragile blue globe, the overall effect of the great universal symphony is not spoiled.

Are The Burst listening? Will they come back to smash our puniness with their cheers and applause when the show reaches its end? These and other questions I have yet to decide. None of us living today will be around for it to be important, so I can probably afford to let such considerations go.

What I am working on, however – the project that keeps me scribbling, composing and tinkling day and night – is delineating some sort of representation of this cosmic work. Some sort of microcosmic, human terms composition that will at least give an inkling of how things really are in this symphonic universe.

Not that anybody's listening…

Arthur's Diary

The first section feels chaotic and demands as many instruments and players as possible. I have been to the local newsagent's because photocopying is quicker than writing everything out by hand and cheaper than printing staves off my second-hand Dell PC. Ideally, I need hundreds of musicians to even approximate the cacophony of the Big Bang. I feel rather like a theatre director trying to conjure up a storm – say, in *King Lear* – and knowing that whatever I come up with can only be a partial success, so much less than having the real thing.

But I must at least try, even if only on the page. George Martin had an orchestra playing to their limit to create the crescendo at the end of The Beatles' *A Day in the Life*. They worked their way up to it. In *Music from the Spheres*, there is no build-up; we have to drop straight in. Ears may bleed. If I'm able to employ sub-sonics, the very walls may fall like at Jericho; people may vomit or have their internal organs ruptured. In the name of artistic endeavour and truthful representation.

If anyone chooses to listen to the rest – if anyone survives the first three minutes – they will be amazed at the creativity and variety taught to us by The Burst. I am, of course, condensing this part from its probable thirteen billion years or so to roughly a mere hour in modern terms. I heard some semi-famous author on Radio Four the other night – a specialist in short stories, the non-commercial fool – and he suggested the skill wasn't what to include but what to leave out. I think I understand his point now.

I'm tired. But I have so much music in my head that I can't sleep. If I ever finish this piece, will I finally find rest?

Enough for now.

Arthur's Diary

I had another thought about the opening. Why not request that the audience participate from the very start? We need to make the noise of that primal explosion, so it's all hands to the pump as soon as the conductor's baton descends. Do your best; do your worst. Scream, stamp your feet, rip out the seats, riot. Start from the tiniest ball you can make and expand, EXPAND and spread out – take the sound and the energy, oh yes the energy, out from the auditorium into the surrounding streets. Indeed, *create* the environment as you progress outwards, that's the ticket, that's how it all worked in the beginning.

Even if I ever finish this hugely difficult opus, I can't think of anywhere that will dare to premiere it. The insurance companies will shake their pinstriped heads and say sorry, this Holkham guy is proposing destruction not creation.

Compromise. The bitter pill we all must always swallow. The only question that ever needs asking is: How big is the dose, nurse?

Arthur's Diary

When I was a lad, I wanted all the usual boyish things: to drive trains, to build bridges, to win Olympic gold. Gradually, all these sweet illusions were taken away from me. When they cancelled my National Service on health grounds after a mere two months, I had to face up to the likelihood of a desk-bound occupation or something within industry but white collar and not too physical. However, I enrolled in a callisthenics evening class and gradually built up my strength. When I tired of industrial chemicals, I devoted myself to teaching and inspiring the future generations.

Why did I bother? They weren't interested in Avogadro's Law or the function of the spleen and thyroid. Sure, I bought myself a cosy home with a sea view – if you take your life in your hands and climb up on the roof to fix the TV aerial – but I can't help feeling that I have wasted so much of my life. And as for the other strand – my interest in music – well, the avenues were cul de sacs and the open doors were mirages.

I had a lovely voice as a boy and snagged all the solos for the school and church choir. I let the organist touch my bare knee and stroke the fair hair on my head and, later, on my thighs. In return, I learned about composition, note values, transcription, holding two or more harmonic or counterpoint pieces in one's head at the same time. I don't remember if he ever masturbated over me; he certainly disappeared off to the toilet round the back of the vestry for inconvenient lengths of time, complaining of 'a little tummy bug'.

I was making up melodies: little hums to amuse myself when it was too rainy to hang around outside or tunes to try out on the assembly hall piano when I was allowed access. I had no real love for crooners, light music or the onrushing wave of rock 'n' roll and pop that was soon to swamp the world in its tinnitus tsunami. I wanted to emulate Mendelssohn or maybe even Wagner. But I was at a crappy little fee-paying school in the Cotswolds and I didn't have the right breeding or the right connections to take my work to the controllers of the orchestras and the dinner-suited chumps running the Third programme. No one was going to listen to me. I could whip up something to play ahead of a carol service or incidental tinkles to complement the village pantomime – that was as far as they let me into the exclusive bubble.

As the years passed, I still scribbled on the staves but accepted that nothing would likely come of this creativity. Clearing out the below stairs cupboard the other day, I was astonished to stumble across so many pages of youthfully exuberant composition. All of this can now feed into my opus, even though I can't recall the provenance of many of the concertos and minuets.

Lately, I have been lying awake coughing for much of the night. I should have quit pipe smoking much earlier but it was one of my few pleasures: to fill the living room with woody, fragrant tobacco smoke like a forest on a spring morning. The doctor has called me in for further tests. I say it's a minor irritation; he believes in emphysema. If he's right, then I must crack on and finish this piece, if only for my own satisfaction. Time is short.

Time is an illusion.

The universe is cold and uncaring.

So what? Deal with it, as the young folk might say.

Info datum deposited by XZ– 43/A:

I've been imprinted with my history block so I know that it was touch and go for a while in the final war between faith and reason. The zealots fought harder, they felt that they had more to believe in, thus they were keener to die for the cause. Only a lucky genocidal breakthrough saw off their final challenge.

We had to grow up. Eradicate the fairy tales, the fables, the hymns, the psalms, the prayers and rituals. Even the words of our calendar – Easter, Christmas, Ascension Day – were retrogressive and undermining. There could be no turning back or even looking back. The only way was forwards… and outwards.

But the way of humankind is seemingly cyclical so that now we have the New Orthodoxy propelling our inevitable dispersal into the uncharted cosmos. The simple mission is to find all relics of The Burst. We have replaced the pantheon of gods of yore with the original super-beings; and I mean literally original. These – what? creatures? gases? consciousnesses? electrical charges? – arrived seemingly fully formed straight after the Big Bang and set about exploring, not to say toying with, the universe. Each planetary orbit is considered to be down to their influence. Each star resonates on a sub-sonic level as the bass orchestration of their grand multi-billion years symphony; each world revolves like a shaken percussive ostinato to add to the overall performance. Nothing in space is random; it is all part of their prehistoric, unfolding composition. The tune is being played out on the grandest, unimaginable scale. Each one of us is the merest micro-fragment of a note that may last a million years.

In olden days societies and civilisations were founded on holy books: the Bible, the Torah, the Qur'an and so forth. Now we base our worldview – our cosmic view – upon the libretto that accompanied an obscure composer's posthumously performed musical suite. That is considered to be some sort of progress.

So we seek The Burst. Maybe they are still there somewhere, listening to their great opera at a safe distance in some alternate universe with a different concept of time.

Maybe they will end it all suddenly and create something else in our stead.

But to my heretical mind this whole search seems retrograde: Humankind seeks gods and masters; please send your curriculum vitae by return and we shall appoint the most experienced candidate available.

Yet still I shall board the starship, operate the Blink Drive, and listen for their killing song.

Interview with Sylvia Simonsen, artistic director for the production:

What have been the key problems involved in staging this production?
I never talk in terms of problems. Issues, maybe, but problems is too negative. Perhaps challenges would serve better here.

To answer your point, the first aspect to consider is the actual opening. It's in the nature of the Big Bang itself to be abrupt, to start out of nothing as it were. The audience has had to be warned to expect an initial shock, a catapulting into a musical representation of the birth of our universe. Holkham's instructions read, "Everything playing at once. Everybody playing everything all at once." This is one of the few orchestral concerts I've ever been involved with staging where the paying public has not been expected to sit in silence; indeed, quite the opposite – scream, slam your seat, stamp your feet, add to the furore. It's not a picnic in the park.

What about the lighting arrangements for the first three minutes?
Good question. We start in darkness – I suppose that's quite conventional. The intrusion of illumination – the burst, if you like – is as abrupt as the music and I have installed a random generator so that bulbs are popping on and off all over the auditorium, with a different configuration each night. Suns being born and dying, worlds and stars coalescing into existence. Novas, supernovas, dust clouds, spiral galaxies. Many of these effects continue into the second part of the symphony.

The whole is quite stroboscopic, to say the least.
True. As much as we have an inclusive, equal access policy – and rightly so – we have had to issue strong warnings that this show is not suitable for anyone who suffers from epilepsy, heart irregularities and any other comparable conditions. It's like the greatest fairground ride ever; except you don't actually move. Quite disorienting, I've found it, all through rehearsals.

What about the characterisation of The Burst? The theoretical original beings of the universe as described – actually, devised – by the composer Arthur Holkham?
You know, most classical concerts one goes to the whole focus is on the music, and rightly so. While you are listening, you might watch the conductor's steady baton movements or focus on the first violinist. Many have said that we need to learn from the extravaganzas of the big rock and pop concerts and make the experience more audio-visual. For this production, I have certainly listened to those voices

The Burst presented the biggest challenge of all. Mythical beings from billions of years ago: how should we show them? Holkham was clear that every echo of godhead from human culture somehow reflects an aspect of these pre-Earth supernatural entities. Therefore, the answer seemed to be to incorporate all and everything. Our projections include every possible interpretation – from the white-bearded Jehovah of the Bible and William Blake to the double helix and atomic creations to gases, energy forms and an invisible absence.

Do you think the notion of The Burst carries some truth?
It's certainly a convincing idea, at least as a theory.

Sylvia, thank you for your time – and good luck with the

production.

Thanks. You're welcome.

Da Capo

Without form. Void. Darkness all around, were such a concept yet invented. Absence. Total absence because there is no space or idea of a space to fill.

No pleasant trickle of musical notes like Beethoven's *Pastoral Symphony*. No tap, tap, tap, tap of the drumstick to indicate that this song must be played in double four time.

Sudden burst into existence. Hence The Burst, that is who we are. The very fabric of the universe is our bodies, our being. We are separate and yet united. We are our own creators. Everything around us is

a toy,

a frippery,

a joy,

a necessity.

Ah, I claim the first doggerel of this cycle.

Ride the crest of the initial uproar. Some are cowering in their seats at the suddenness of the onslaught. Some are attempting to leave the building. They may succeed – we have already created buildings.

We mess around for a while – time is now something that can be considered, maybe even measured. We play – we are still but children, infants even in this new creation, the post-Big Bang universe.

Somewhere below the bellowing orchestra, the screeching woodwind and the cacophonous timpani, there are mutterings from the Festival Hall crowd that this is not music, this is rubbish, mere noise dressed up, the aural equivalent of *The Emperor's New Clothes*.

"Ground-breaking," one wag observes, "it's certainly that. I wouldn't be surprised if this racket causes an earthquake below the Thames, a chasm to swallow up Waterloo station."

Humour delights us. We are still young, even in the cosmic

sense.

Ours it is to set the templates for all the arts and sciences that will sprout from these first three frantic minutes. All that follows after – broader time notions now, see! – shall reflect our primacy. We give and you shall exist on our manna, whether it be feast or crumbs.

Which one of us has the cool idea – which aspect of our unity has the cool idea – of making the whole progress of the universe into a billions of years symphony, I know not. I would like to claim it. Enough that it is my people, the incomparable Burst, first on the scene and imprinted for eternity, who set every planet and star in motion, resonating with their own musical signature, their own unseen stave to adhere to, their own ostinato or riff or back beat to hold, their own tiny role in this grand scheme, the greatest – certainly the longest-lasting – symphony ever to be attempted.

This production is, of course, little more than homage, a microcosmic representation of our pan-galactic glory. Still, it's nice to be acknowledged, even if half the audience walked out before the rarer elements were created. Nice one, Arthur… whoever you were.

Planet Suite Rip-off Fails to Appeal
By your arts correspondent, Toby Morey.

It was billed as a musical miracle; it was a musical mess. And, frankly, a waste of taxpayers' money that could have perhaps gone to fund a few more inner city DJ and studio schemes or helped put a young indie band on the map.

Music from the Spheres? If you were expecting balloons – well, the racket would have burst them. A spinning disco ball like a sparkly planet in the heavens? No, this music was dull, crashing and hellish. If you craved the *Moonlight Sonata* or *Fly Me to the Moon* by Sinatra – forget it. Lunar? This was lunacy.

More percussionists than a tinnitus convention.

Crazy instruments designed by crackpots and sounding worse than actual cracked pots. And that's when you could actually discern some sort of attempt at music emanating from the orchestra pit. Yes, 'from the pit' just about says it all.

As for the sorry tale that accompanied this cacophony… Even von Daniken or David Icke would have balked at this weird narration about a race of superior beings – gods, if you will – having been created moments after the Big Bang and treating the universe as some sort of cosmic playground. Ah, but there we have it. The Arts Council, indeed the Arts establishment itself, has always rewarded the unashamedly childish. And this was the late Arthur Holkham's messy staves of pure infantilism, given the chin stroking treatment regularly reserved for those who open a piano lid but don't play or who paint one slab of colour onto a large canvas and call it *Reflection on the Impossibility of Being Human* or some such pretentious guff.

Listen, lovely readers, I was being paid good money to listen to this drivel and so I stayed to the bitter end – although there were colleagues on sister papers who made righteously for the Festival Hall bar within three minutes, and who can blame them? At the cessation of this aural torture, as the players and singers and technicians stood in the sudden big bang of light to take their bow to non-existent applause, I was overcome with a debilitating wave of sorrow. Not occasioned by any emotional intensity on the part of the music, I hasten to add. No, I felt sorry for the wasted man hours spent rehearsing and preparing the show. And for the hour and a half (that's a whole England football match worth of playing time!) of my life that I'll never get back.

Music from the Spheres claims to be the true musical history of the cosmos. Holst has already had a decent stab at this, boys. Give me *Jupiter – the Bringer of Joy* any day. Blimey, I'd even prefer ninety minutes of Radio One. Or, God forbid, *The X Factor Live Tour*! Music from the Spheres? Music for Eggheads, more like. Avoid at all costs.

The Perils of Pentavir

Genesis

In the beginning was The Five.

And The Five was without equal and was static and perfect. But the universe itself is ever changing and so The Five became the five that we know of as the Five Founders, through an essentially simple but unique and revolutionary process of cell division. And verily did the Five Founders begin our civilisation on the moonless, ring-free, beautifully glittering central jewel in the string necklace of the original solar system.

And God or Nature or The Burst – if any of them ever existed, which many of us doubt – saw this world and knew that it was good.

As did the original inhabitants of Pentavir, the beautiful world between Mars and Jupiter, faintly licked by the sun but warmed by internal volcanism and shrouded by semi-permeable clouds like diamanté curtains. The people grew tall and fair or dark or creamy coffee coloured and knew not divisions based upon skin pigmentation. Art and science flourished alongside a mysticism and spirituality which never cemented into the tired rituals and thought-limitation of organised religion. The holy texts were also the holy frescoes and holy equations and mantras. And they all spoke of or delineated a world destined to represent a golden age. They all pictured a world based upon the five spokes of the star, each constituent point inter-dependent upon all the others and revolving slowly so that there was no up or down as such and no vertex of the five star could ever be said to be on top. If any corner showed weakness, all others would rush to help and strengthen and the sacred astra would be preserved and flourish anew. The years of plenty would be almost numberless. The people would live with song in their hearts, bread in their bellies and bright sparks in their imaginations.

Long live the glory that is Pentavir.

Live long on Pentavir.

And yet a re-evaluation of the original texts brought about a gradually infiltrating miasma of melancholy as it became clear that nothing could last forever, not even this Arcadian civilisation of peace and prosperity. The doubts ate into the minds: the notion of future doom took hold and gradually held sway. And like all self-fulfilling prophecies, it made itself happen. Soon co-existence became conflict of interest. Neighbour became competitor. Scythes and ploughshares became swords and pistols. Within barely five to the power of five generations, the whole planet was set upon a course for total destruction. Everybody knew this; nobody knew how to stop this.

Nobody succeeded in stopping it.

Genesis Books Two and Three

Millennia later, the narrow-minded astronomers and physicists of fragile Earth maintain that there is not enough existent debris within the asteroid belt to support such an idea as a fifth planet but we blinkered Earth-bound scientists have not yet taken on the notion of sizeable inter-planetary drift. The leftover bits from the cosmos-shaking explosion that did for poor Pentavir were mostly sent towards the barrier at the edge of the solar system. Indeed, they strengthened its composition and interfered with its expansion for several aeons.

Mars hangs dead and lifeless. Venus is not the green, lush forest of Perelandra but has already been over-cooked. Earth is our final chance and we have almost blown that.

Our crazy, mixed-up hero – astronaut Simon Cooper – sits in his lonely garret pondering the possibility of either a benign Creator or visitors from elsewhere kick-starting human progress and yet is troubled by childish remnants of myth and fairy tale and Bible stories that can't be literally true. Beyond all pondering upon the meaning of life and the purpose, if any, to the whole of existence, Simon Cooper simply waits and wishes to somehow be reunited with Jane Wylie or the space nereid Miranda, whilst the rest of the world casually gets on with its inevitable career along the path to self-destruction.

Simon never got as far as Pluto – which is probably a good thing now that the poor old dark ball of rock has been downgraded to minor planet or dwarf planet status. Not allowed into the club with the big boys. Given the old, cold shoulder by King Jove and Co.

Simon travelled through the asteroid belt but he never fully explored the questionable notion of the lost fifth planet. The guys back at Mission Control were having none of it – just a space hazard, a bunch of rocks and dust on the astral super-highway.

Wrong. Pentavir was once the fifth planet, located between Mars and Jupiter as the jewel of our solar system. Pentavir: the place, the idea. Pentavir: The last of the rocky havens, the source of all our wishes, memories, hopes and desires.

What we call the asteroid belt circles in an ellipse just the way a planet would. The actual planet that once orbited there – Pentavir – has been atomised into a perilous girdle of debris. Naturally, some rocks are bigger than others. Some may fall out of orbit and trouble explorers or even neighbouring planets. Keep an eye out, one could come and wipe out the Pentagon and the Empire State Building at any moment.

A new Internet-based theory begs to suggest that, on an infinitesimally slow scale, the disparate stones are actually seeking recombination. The original Paradise can yet be re-created.

A Call to the Troops

And in those days a decree went out from Geezer Augustus that all men shall be taxed in order to raise an army to represent their side in the battle to the death. And each man, woman, child, sprog and hermaphrodite was required to return to the palace or laboratory of their birth so that the taxing could begin.

We want your money, we want your loyalty, we want your blood for our transfusions and your spare skin for our grafting. And each was taxed in correlation with their ability to give so that a fission of fusiliers could take their rightful place at each spoke of the agreed battlefields. This was the most civilised and organised war in the long and mythically glorious history of Pentavir; and yet, also the technologically most kill-efficient and bloodiest. All hail the Five Founders, the First Born of our planet, and let the determined slaughter commence.

Science Versus Mythology

Whereas Earth geography is based upon the Christian cross with its four directions of North, South, East and West, the Pentavirians mapped their flat representation of a spherical world with five points like the star or the pentagram. Indeed, the star superimposed over a circle, which holds apparent evil or witchcraft powers on sad, neurotic Earth, began life simply as a quick sketch to stand for the fifth planet, just the way the astrologers have their cryptic symbols for Taurus, Cancer, Capricorn and so forth. The demonic aspect is a mixed-up memory of Pentavir's ultimate fate. The early Christians adapted what they could of the so-called pagan religions – co-opting Yuletide as a handy time to celebrate Christmas, for example – but anything that didn't fit they immediately classed as the work of the devil. The cross, the tree of life and death, the perpendicular and right angles fitted their template beautifully. Ninety-degree angles and straight up, down and across fitted their mind set so much better than seventy-two degrees and a confusion of inter-linked almost-diagonals.

Some scholars have suggested that Pentavir's ultimate fate was also down to numbers and a basic conflict of symbolic piety. The five armies fought fiercely and unquestioningly; the apparent masters worked relentlessly behind the scenes negotiating, setting up and scuppering deals. At a crucial point in the war for supremacy it became clear that there were actually *two* loose alliances within this conflict, not five separate co-existent interest groups. Five into two simply wouldn't go and destruction became inevitable.

The belief persists that each great civilisation carries within it the seed of its own destruction and all records and speculation about past events seems to bear this out. Every evil empire has its day but later dies. Each attempt at paradise is doomed to failure. Utopia and Dystopia alike shall fall to the hands of time and the grasping fingernails of entropy.

The elders and intellects of Pentavir realised a little too late that their great civilisation – the template for Olympus, Atlantis and all other heavenly mythologies – was doomed by its current state of reductionism. Whereas before we had held Five as the true number of the universe, now we were taking it down to the base binary, the either / or, on / off dualism which would dominate all Earthly thought for centuries to come. We were losing our higher abilities, regressing, undergoing a not so subtle atrophy within our thinking. This was our doom.

And even those who were right now planning a possible off-world escape might only end up by taking the new, simple-minded thinking with them.

Deterrents and Determinism

Poor Pentavir. A rich and flourishing history becomes a gradual lurch towards over-population; asset stripping; over-consumption of natural resources; ethnic strife; and stockpiling of weapons of mass destruction. Each side now holds what is considered to be the ultimate deterrent. An uneasy balance is maintained. We have the power to destroy ourselves and our heavenly planet many times over… but so do our neighbours / our opponents / our sworn enemies. Which of the five digits will be first to twitch and launch? For surely one resolve must crack… will crack eventually.

The World Council meets in semi-secret session on the central island of Atlantis. An escape plan is discussed. A ship shall be built, carrying the best of our race: the pioneers who will re-plant our seed of hope and start again. An ark into space comprising crew, passengers, fuel, supplies, domestic animals, crops, medicine, adaptive technology and DNA.

The what, the how and the why are quickly dealt with.

Which leaves:

Who? Big sticking point this: everyone wants a ride out of here.

Where? We've got our eyes on the third planet. It's a little warmer and the gravity is a touch stronger, which will make us sluggish until we adjust, but it's the only viable option.

When? As soon as possible, before our inevitable self-destruction renders any escape too late. There is really no time to lose.

The Earthly Book of Numbers
Selected Chapters and Verses

The inhabitants of Pentavir had long since been blessed with the requisite technology and knowledge to know their planet as the fifth great stone out from the sun. Some of Earth's more extrapolative scholars have conjectured – on no surviving evidence – that the inhabitants of the fabled lost planet latterly based all their undertaking around the number five. Thus: counting and monetary systems worked in fives rather than tens; the perfect building was deemed to include pentagonal faces; and even relationships and family units gravitated towards varying degrees of pentism.

Everything was done for five, in praise of five and because of five.

*

So, what do we meek little Earthlings have for five? What remains on this sorry, second rate, third planet, start again, last chance saloon world?

We could just as easily have taken the fingers of *one* hand and said "Five and then start again" rather than combining both appendages. The Roman V rather than the more troublesome X. Indeed, if we go with the prevailing view that the universe is predicated upon binary oppositions – life / death, male / female, left / right, yin / yang and so on – surely we should only acknowledge the fixed fingers of one hand and, like Robert Mitchum's preacher in *Night of the Hunter*, consider the parallel as the enemy – love and hate fighting each other eternally in a bid for ultimate supremacy, but based upon the five digits of the human hand.

Five senses.

Five Alive.

High Five.

Give me five.

Take Five.

The Jackson Five

The Dave Clark Five.

The Famous Five.

Five go mad in Dorset.

Instructions from the Pentagon.

Spells cast within the pentagram.

The star and the starfish.

But not the snowflake.

Five refreshing fruit flavours.

The Saturn V.

Five seconds till lift off.

The first prime number to be preceded by a multiple.

Five petalled flowers and five pointed leaves: the rose, the lily, the vine.

A key integer in the Fibonacci sequence: the pattern that creates the magic of the mollusc and the snail shell.

The combination of two and three, the conflicting ideas of the old and new.

Da Vinci depicted Man via the pentacle – the head at the top, the outstretched arms and legs bringing the number of the human to five.

The four elements plus the guiding principle that raises us above the common herd. Thus we once consisted of: Spirit, Air, Fire, Water, and Earth.

Oh Earth, I believe we are losing all spirit or soul and our lives are now reduced to the material. Nothing remains of greater meaning, all is downgraded to the merely mundane: the next breath, exchange of heat, a necessary drink or a welcome place to crawl into.

The Holy Five is the four cardinal points plus the centre. This is the nearest we might get these days to the essential numbering of the lost world.

The absent quintessence of being.

But not enough. We have shucked off so much of the fifth planet heritage that now it seems a mere myth, a simple science fiction wish-fulfilment fantasy. Everything is about the two – black and white, good and evil – or even the four – fire, water, earth and air – rather than the troublesomely pointed star of the five. It is perhaps this distance from our cultural beginning which leaves us so at sea.

Free us oh Ancients from this mental tyranny of the either/or! Bring us back to the spread, spatulate palate of thumb, index, middle, ring, little and by doing this bring about the consequent broadening fork of life choices.

We should seek to remake Pentavir. It was clearly everywhere we remember – Atlantis, Tir-na-Nog, Avalon, the Dreamtime, Eden.

(*Here endeth the lesson*)

Exodus – Movement of Five's People

And the word was sent out from all corners and to all quadrants of the doomed planet Pentavir that we were facing the end of days and yet there existed the one seed of hope. Even now the spaceship *Pandora* was being readied for its maiden and only flight – to take the chosen flowers of our race towards a hopeful new beginning on the evocative blue and white marble of the third planet. We'd skip beyond the obvious close target of Mars – they had their own inhabitants and issues to deal with; let's go somewhere wild and untamed with creatures who could soon fall under our dominion.

The gravity is a bit strong, admittedly, and this may slow our imposition of the new order. Have faith; we'll get used to it. We're going to take this place and make all other species succumb to our will. So we've messed up here on our home world – we'll learn our lesson, we won't do it again, will we? Will we?

And we'll remember the home planet even after the inevitable cataclysm. We'll know it as the Camelot, the Gilgamesh, the Paradise of old. We shall hold memories of the Great Old Ones. They came from the sky… *we* came from the sky.

There are those who think the escape craft should head outwards to Jove. But it's dark there and stormy. We'd need a bigger craft in order to transport the world-transforming apparatus. There just isn't time. This whole place is going to blow soon.

Seed the stars, I hear you suggest. As if! The stars are not suns, but mere distortions upon the inner surface of the giant bubble which encloses our beloved solar system.

Many philosophers postulate that there must be an *outside* to this enclosed spherical space. Just suppose these neo-heretics are correct, what then? Have you ever punctured a bubble or a balloon? Exactly – the whole shebang explodes into nothingness.

If anyone is to survive this Armageddon, we cannot take the chance of destroying everything and causing the whole of eternity to implode upon us. It's bad enough that we shall inevitably destroy our home planet, we must ensure that we do not take Sol and his family down with us.

Others have categorically stated that space is expanding ever outwards but *slowly*, so that the solar system grows infinitesimally larger even as we watch, but that's all there is.

At length, the *Pandora* is almost completely built, stocked with supplies, fully fuelled and ready to blast off. Do you want to be aboard? Of course you do. Are you likely to secure a berth on this last fling of our Atlantean civilisation? No, pal, not a prayer.

Reductive Numbers

So much of our perception of the universe is down to our competency with numbers. All our recent technological advances are essentially digital. Everything we know and everything we invent can be expressed as a formula. Our computers turn every strand of DNA, every exchange of electrons, every word of love and hate into a string of sequenced digits. Some long for the days of analogue but, this side of the self-inflicted apocalypse, there is no going back to the number-free mindset.

Numbers Three

Furthermore, it is our choice of numbers – these tools that both aid us to understand the universe yet limit our parameters for thought – which shapes our thinking and, by extension, our very existence on this doomed blue and white planet. So much of our culture is rooted in dualism, the power of numéro deux. Light or dark, alive or dead, Religion or Science, Creation or Evolution. Purpose or pointlessness.

Given our position in relation to the burning ball of hydrogen, three ought to be a more popular choice down here on the third stone from the sun. The trio and the triad. The eternal triangle. Guitar, bass, drums. Three in a bed. The Jimi Hendrix Experience.

Some philosophers have sought to express three as the magic number which overcomes the partitioning occasioned by the duality of in or out, with us or against us. Thus, thesis and antithesis may be combined or conquered and overcome by the beauty of synthesis. If only…

Three rears its head in the peculiar conceptual twist of the Holy Trinity, the spiritual waltz time that brings God the Father impregnating the Virgin through the agency of himself The Holy Spirit to produce himself as God the Son. The mind boggles.

Popular culture has embraced three options only to the following, phone-in extent:

Which British author wrote the classic science fiction disaster novel *The Drowned World?* Was it Brian Aldiss, J. G. Ballard or Arthur C. Clarke?

Call this premium rate number and you could win a trip to the Arctic ice floes before they melt and disappear forever.

Calls cost £1.50, of which at least 75p will be donated to The Polar Bear Preservation Society. Mobile costs vary. Digital viewers – as opposed to *optical* viewers? – may press the red button for an onscreen menu. Or simply text the word 'DROWNED' followed by A for Aldiss, B for Ballard or C for Clarke.

Numbers Four

Four we love as the underpinning sum of deductive logic – so I put two and two together and came up with… Western popular music is rooted in four beats to the bar, four to the floor, double four time. All British written test multiple choice exam papers from SATS onwards offer the four choices.

Circle the correct answer in pen or pencil.

Simon Cooper encountered the space nereids in orbit around Jupiter; Saturn; Uranus; Neptune.

The title of this book is:

The Planets, The Planet Suite, To The Planets, The Planets Tout de Suite.

(Note to examiners: Accept any other clear method of indication, such as a tick. Award one mark per question.)

Science Versus Science

Speaking for the Opposition, please give your full attention to His Pentasticness, Colonel Peyton Five Hand Joints:

"Gentlemen, we are limiting our options by heading inwards towards the fourth, third or second planet. This notion that the solar system is all that exists is a convenient, reductive limitation on thought and action, demanding obedience to our current rulers and the maintenance of the status quo. And the end of such helmeted thinking… is the end of our civilisation in an inevitable, ultimate conflict of the sort we are now facing.

"But what proof do we really have of this cosily limited consideration of the cosmos? This view of the stars as simply points of light; and all our technical readings apparently mere distortions caused by the bubble or barrier at the edge of the known?

"This is irrational, wish fulfilment at best. Or, in layman's terms: Poppycock, I say.

"Everything was created by one giant explosion and, even within the early years of the universe, life flourished: with a superhuman species we have come to know as The Burst. This is the true root of our tales of gods, our myths of golden ages and the long descent since. After the first fireworks of the Big Bang's opening three-minute salvo, everything was bound to be a let-down, a cooling off, a diminuendo after such a hot opening number.

"The Burst, heavenly men of action, didn't sit around cold, dark Pluto saying to themselves, 'Oh, I don't think I want to go on any further, I'm nearly at the edge of everything.' The whole macrocosm was their plaything. The Andromeda Nebula, the Milky Way, the black holes all echo with their long-departed but significant passage.

"I despair that the strictly heliocentric, people-glorifying business so many of my contemporaries indulge in makes us no better than children. This quasi-solipsism hasn't saved our planet and won't save anybody else's.

"The truth, of course, may be that we are mere specks, microscopic and microcosmic in universal terms; but the important difference is that there is a universe out there. And that's where our escape craft should be headed.

"With me aboard."

- Peyton Five Hand Joints (Colonel)

Numbers Five

Here on Earth in these desperate modern days, there is not so much call for five but the memory of our previous existence on lost Pentavir still lingers in some of the staff training course feedback sheets and low-level psychological profiling.

Please tick one box:

I use classical music as a relaxant:

Always, Most of the Time, Sometimes, Hardly Ever, Never.

I would say today's seminar has been:

Very Useful, Quite Useful, Useful, Not Particularly Useful, Absolute Crap.

Please circle one answer before you join the queue to board *The Modern Pandora*.

From The Holy Book of Merchandise

Keep the faith.

Reject the new heresy.

Show your support for an infinite universe, an ancient universe, a universe created in a great flash of light.

For just four pentas, be the trendiest on your apex by sporting our newly re-designed anti-static cape bearing the slogan, 'The Burst were the First!'

Available now in all sizes.

Revelations Part One

And in those days there were shepherds out in their fields tending to their sheep. And lo, in a blaze of light and glory, there appeared an angle before them. Not an *angel* but verily an *angle*. And though they were lowborn, uneducated and pretty close to being social pariahs, what with the lingering ovine smells about their clothes and appendages, they knew the holy angle for one of the vertices of the everlasting pentacle and they were sore afraid.

"Fear!" proclaimed the angle. "In fact, be very frightened because I bring you tidings of great ill. In Pent-Le Hem this very day is hatched the plan of our race's final destruction. Ye shall find the killing weapon atop a Saturn V rocket wrapped in metal casing. It's no longer the issue as to whether one side or another will ever launch these weapons of total destruction but, simply, a matter of when. Already the great and good – and those not so great and good but rich, powerful and influential enough – are taking to the contour couches of the escape craft which shall be known as '*Pandora*' and will forever be recalled as our lady of hope amidst the froth of evil. Humanity – I do not say human*kind* – shall survive because of our foresight and our need to know."

Forthwith did the elder of the shepherds rise to question the celestial visitor and did say, "Why, O great angle, oh heavenly corner of intersecting and combining straight lines, are you bringing us this wretched news? In short, what's the point?"

Cue much backslapping from his bearded colleagues at such unexpected nocturnal fun with a pun.

All at once there was a multitude of siren calls and a gnashing of alarms and the doomed fifth planet of paradise shook upon its axis. A tremor before the fatal heart attack. A convulsion before the final fit.

And there came a brightness which dazzled the lowly shepherds and reduced them to prostrate pilgrims upon the half-chewed grass. And the angle revealed its true glory with the demonic revelation of a full spinning pentacle that hypnotised and engulfed all who saw its beauty. "You, my friends," spake the angle, "have the honour of boarding the escape rocket. As ballast."

Revelations Part Five

A new Internet-based, academically dismissed but naggingly compelling theory begs to suggest that, on an infinitesimally slow scale, the disparate stones that we Earthlings know as the asteroid belt are actually seeking recombination. Or – heretical view – original fusion.

Let's take this proposal and run with it. This means that the ultimate twist in the tale may be that Pentavir is not so much a memory as an *aspiration*.

One day we shall make Paradise, not rediscover it but create it.

Pentavir is where we should be headed. Time is not strictly linear. We have not been expelled from Eden – we just haven't fully formed it as a realistic, practical, achievable concept yet. All our myths, all our religions are distorted reflections of the future we might attain.

Or, given the state of our world and our warring civilisations, the future we might not.

The End

DVD Extras

That First Book Feeling by Allen Ashley

Author's Note: The original scheduled publication date for *The Planet Suite* was October 1996 and, indeed, a few proof copies became available in late 1996. The official publication date for the book was put back to 1ˢᵗ March 1997, but not until after this article appeared in *Zene issue 9, Autumn 1996*.

My first full-length book *The Planet Suite* is due from TTA Press in October this year. It actually started life just as a vague urge to write a short story about sex, sea and space. This coalesced into the exploration of bodily orifices known as *Seven Rides to Venus*. I wrote the story in July 1993 and it was published in *The Third Alternative* a year later. It was a breakthrough piece for me: 'postmodernist' structure; 'slipstream' content; intensely personal but still with a general enough element to achieve publication. I had several ideas left over – tentatively known as *The Further Exploration of Space* – and mooted the idea of a sequel… which I duly wrote and sent to Andy Cox. And I still had loads of unused notes. I'm not a writer who is ever going to write massive character studies or family sagas; what's important to me is the idea(s), the 'what if?', which is why I've always been drawn at least to the fringes of science fiction. I'd somehow unlocked the cranial floodgates and by January 1995 Andy had given me the green light to produce a collection of linked stories relating to the planets of the solar system.

From April 1995 the book suddenly gathered momentum. I had story three – *The Last Martian Artefact* – accepted for the ill-fated *New Statesman* anthology and decided to set myself a timetable of writing one *Planet Suite* story every two months. Maybe this sounds over-generous to myself. Certainly I always respond well to deadlines. I felt two months was realistic because it gave me one month for writing and the other for rewriting and chucking out. It also allowed time to have those necessary weeks 'off' when health, the day job or the usual domestics became too important. I was looking at writing a total of about a dozen average length stories. After the frantic buzz of *Martian* I felt that I could genuinely keep the obsession going for another twelve to eighteen months.

At least I was not faced with the mixed blessing of turning out two (paying) novels a year but, even so, I had spells of writer's block just like everybody else. My ways of dealing with it are to chuck down any old rubbish ('write my way out of the crisis') because I can always rewrite later; or to knock out a few reviews, notes, ideas for amending rejected stories, or anything else that's not 100% new creation. Sometimes I *chose* to work on other stories. At these times I experienced a curious sense of guilt telling me I ought to have been speculating on the frozen seas of Neptune or Saturn's magical rings at every grabbed writing moment. Of course, there are times when the fire's inside you so much that you're scared there isn't enough time to get everything down on paper. I was pretty flexible in my writing habits beforehand but *The Planet Suite* forced me to seize every opportunity – lunchtimes, half hours after work, sleepless Saturday mornings when your body clock's still on weekday schedule, etc. – and to blast ideas onto a screen or into a Dictaphone as well as more conventional pen and paper methods. Get the ideas and the stories down however you can, however you have to; it's always worth staying up till half past two rather than putting a scene off till the next day. Take it from me: I've got the bags under the eyes to prove it.

In calling the book *The Planet Suite* I'm making an obvious link with Gustav Holst's symphony and by December 1995 I had decided I wanted to write a whole (and almost wholly fictitious) piece about the composer – *First World Tour*. Like Holst, I'm more interested in the mythological aspects of the planets than the absolute facts. Serendipitous to Andy Darlington's excellent *Planets Project* in *The Zone*, my stories are something of an attempt to reclaim that SF Golden Age sense of wonder when we hoped the planets were exotic but habitable – undiscovered rainforests or a new Antarctica. Holst's

Neptune The Mystic is one of my ten favourite tracks. Don't tell anyone, but I'm more likely to be listening to 60s psychedelia than popular classics. In essence, what I'm saying is: be as original as you can, bring out what makes your work special, pattern the book your own way even if there's a nodding acquaintance to other artists and influence.

My actual writing methods have evolved over the years. Although I'm still a perfectionist and would like to get everything mentally flawless and in proper order before writing one word (I'm told Flaubert was like this), I don't go from A to Z during the creative process and I'm often faced with 40+ pieces of paper containing varying amounts of scribble from the last few weeks which I then have to edit / rewrite / throw out / add up into something of a coherent whole. Maybe it sounds scatty but it works for me – and twice during *The Planet Suite* it left me with enough material for two discrete stories where I'd started with just the one.

Research is another important aspect of my work. I find myself doing more and more – it can quickly become the whole of your reading! For example, I read loads of creation myths for my story *Helios*. Eventually I was immersed enough in the subject that I was able to concoct three of my own, which was the desired outcome.

This 'projected' novel has taken over three years to write and get into print. Of course, it's all worth it and, yes, there's a part of me which wishes to pack in the day job and write full time – but who's to say I'd make a living or actually produce any more work than now? It's the 90s writer's conundrum. A lot of authors are under pressure to produce a novel every year but even with an advance of, say, £5000, they've then got to chase further work and make ends meet by knocking out intellectually challenged spot articles for mass market magazines and supplements. Pressure here, stress there, doubtful quality everywhere!

But I still have the dream that goes something like: Andy sells the rights on to Penguin / Harper Collins / etc… I get commissioned to write another novel… David Lynch pays £50,000 for the cult film rights to my unfilmable stories… you know this dream world, you've all lingered there!

In the summer of 1994 I had a manic five-day spell of sun, storms and total writing in a caravan at Cromer (the model for 'Shiplea' in the book) and I want it again and again! As Jim Morrison said, "We want the world and we want it now."

A Few Reviews from the 1990s

"Any novel that sails the rough seas between mainstream and genre is to be welcomed – this is the course for the future! Allen Ashley, with Gustav Holst aboard, keeps a firm hold on the compass." – Brian W. Aldiss

"A work of genius" – Rhys Hughes in *Touchpaper*

"A remarkable combination of the choreographed and the bacchanal." – *Event*

"Here is a bulletin of timeless importance from the talented British writer, Allen Ashley. **The Planet Suite** offers an innovative tour of the Solar system, along the infinite frontiers of human imagination. Drawing on classical mythology, Golden Age SF and contemporary Fantasy, Ashley's creation is full of literary ingenuity and genre allusions. It is tempting to wax lyrical about **The Planet Suite**… No synopsis could do it justice. I can only say that if you're fed up with derivative SF / Fantasy epics, and would like to read something that may renew your faith in publishing as an innovative medium, **The Planet Suite** is highly recommended." – Tony Lee in *Starburst*

"Though time and space elide, and though action may be realistic, fantastic or surreal, a plot of the simplest and most universal kind emerges: a childhood / adolescent love is lost and endlessly resought. The young characters… are re-cast in various analogical roles, realistically in those of prosaic adulthood and fantastically as astronauts and generation pilots… imaginatively innovative… the fun, the satire and the correlatively disjointed human story pull chaos towards a comprehensible ideative unity." – K. V. Bailey in *Vector*

Original Back Page Blurb

Each successive astronaut has gazed back and found our magic marble a little less blue. The Moon landings offered a promise which is never likely to be delivered. Maybe the only solar system we can explore is as a concept and collection of myths, ideas and images of Venus, Mars, Mercury and so forth; to wit:

the planets in our heads…

A tour de force of memory, mythology and astronomy, this is the most audacious debut novel of the 1990s.

Spaced-Out in the Slipstream

An Interview with Allen Ashley
By Roger Keen

First published in *Dragon's Breath 46 / 47*, New Year 1998, Pigasus Press. Reproduced as printed apart from one amendment of a slight factual error, which was my fault – Allen

More than any other 'slipstream' writer, Allen Ashley has made a point of advertising his affiliation to the movement. With his boldly experimental stories, his lively, sometimes tongue-in-cheek contributions to the slipstream debate, and the recent publication of *The Planet Suite*, a slipstream novel, he has become a conspicuous figure, and at the same time he seems comfortable out there on the sometimes lonely cutting edge.

One could view his work as resembling that of an abstract painter. There were the naturalistic roots in fairly conventional short stories appearing in such magazines as PEEPING TOM and the now ceased FANTASY TALES. But then there were also more challenging melting-pot type experimental pieces showing up in the likes of BACK BRAIN RECLUSE. And eventually there was the emergence of a formal, distinctive non-naturalistic style, most in evidence in his stories for Andy Cox's THE THIRD ALTERNATIVE.

Of course his seminal *7 Rides To Venus* (TTA 3) was undoubtedly the most important, signalling a breakthrough into new realms of creativity. It blended lyrical, beautifully written SF with childhood reminiscences and cosmic philosophy in a narrative fusion which transcended and blurred the usual genre boundaries. The piece was well received and considered to be a definitive slipstream product. So what had set Allen going in this new direction?

"I'd been trying for several years to move away from a standard linear structure, and also to have faith in exploring things that were very personal to me… rather than trying to write yet another Frankenstein story, or yet another Dracula story, or ghost story with a twist in the tale.

"I didn't want to copy anyone – I wanted to write exactly like myself, because ultimately if I'm going to have any success or make any mark as a writer, or feel real satisfaction as a writer, I'm going to do it by finding my own voice."

After completing *7 Rides…*, Allen had several ideas left over and embarked on a second – related – story: *Jupiter and Beyond*, continuing the mix of space exploration, scenes from the childhood backgrounds of the main characters, Simon and his love Jane Wylie, and other more freeform improvisations sections. Having done two of the planets, a natural structure for an extended work suggested itself, involving a trip around the Solar system and various interludes.

Allen had approached Andy Cox with the proposal that he publish a collection of Allen's stories, but initially Andy wasn't keen, saying that single author collections rarely did any business. But the idea of a themed, unified collection of pieces appealed to Andy; he agreed to the project and *The Planet Suite* was born. By the time Allen had written the third piece, *The Last Martian Artefact*, he felt he knew where he was going with the work as a whole.

"What one is trying to reclaim as a writer is a view of the world as a fantastic place, a magical place, a place that can surprise you. That's something I think one can have as a child, and it's a theme which runs throughout '*The Planet Suite*'. It's not just recapturing childhood innocence, though, it's about trying to see beyond the nitty-gritty, the dirty realism – and that's why I'm drawn towards slipstream writing because you can have events which don't stand up to empirical testing."

Venus is depicted as very much a new Garden of Eden, with a lush life-sustaining climate; and Mars is (perhaps) inhabited by a sinister hairless all-male race who incite outbreaks of Reds-under-the-bed style paranoia on earth. Allen constantly stresses that the content of the work is not to be taken literally:

"It's not hard-SF, it's not *Red Mars*, it's not Arthur C. Clarke… I didn't want to be imprisoned by current scientific knowledge – having to deal with the planets in the Solar system with the scientific knowledge that we have, having to deal with the fact that the atmosphere would kill you, the pressure would kill you, the temperature would kill you, and really they're uninviting! I wanted to restore this pulp Science Fiction idea, this Edgar Rice Burroughs idea, this early Ray Bradbury idea… I wanted to go backwards."

And part of that backward journey involved an exploration of the creation myths of many cultures for the 'Helios' section of the book. This led onto the invention of some completely new ones, as well as asking some hard questions about our current 'creation mythology', as embodied in state of the art physics.

"I'm very interested in creation myths. I find myself making biblical references, and surprising myself by making them. I went to church school when I was a primary school child, and I went to Sunday school for two or three years, but that's about it – unless you count my Religious Education O' Level! At some level a lot of these ideas have seeped down into my unconscious. I couldn't tell you exactly what I believe. I'm not satisfied with the theory of the Big Bang; I think it raises questions which maybe we'll never answer. I mean, I look for reasons – why was there a Big Bang? What happened before? If you're imagining that everything that's around us now and everything that's light years beyond was compressed into a space smaller than that red light on your Dictaphone. Why? Did someone push it all together? I can't get my head around it. It's too much to comprehend. But I'm interested, and a lot of the impetus in *The Planet Suite* was exploring ideas, raising questions, not necessarily delivering answers."

But as well as 'heavy' stuff like the meaning of everything, *The Planet Suite* also contains playful and humorous interludes, where, one might say, slipstream really lets its hair down. How could a book about such a subject – and with such a title – not pay homage to Gustav Holst, the prime provider of our soundtrack of the Solar system? In *First World Tour* Allen gives Holst an alternative rock 'n' roll biography, dragging him through the drug culture of the sixties into the music biz present of interactive CD-ROMs and quadraphonic concerts.

"I felt very comfortable writing that, because a natural way of writing for me is to write in this diaristic style. So I took Gustav Holst and I threaded in realistic details of his life – I mean, he really did fall off a stage in Reading, and things like that – but I put the typical 90s view on things – sort of post-psychoanalysis and reconstructed history – and cast him as this acid casualty… because it was fun! I like to have fun. There's things like this Billy Graham type character comes up to him and says, 'We can invent the light show with this: The Planets! Yeah, man! I can really see this as a Pink Floyd kind of thing!' – thirty years before the Pink Floyd was born. Yeah, I was having fun with chronology…"

Humour – in particular ironic, knowing humour – has featured in Allen's work before. His *Thin Man's Guide to Slipstream* – an hilarious list of the 'requirements' of a slipstream exponent – caused quite a stir when it appeared in THE THIRD ALTERNATIVE. It contained advice such as: profess not to watch any soaps unless they're directed by David Lynch; and: only read the letters columns in genre magazines. Some loved it while others felt he was ridiculing a serious subject. Whatever the case, the memory of it brings a big smile to his face.

"At that stage I thought the (slipstream) debate was taking itself a little bit too seriously. People were jumping up on their high horses and falling out with each other, and yet really they were trying to do the same stuff. So I was trying to take the heat out. It maybe caused offence to one or two people, and yet I've spoken to them all since. It's like Jewish people will tell you that they can tell Jewish jokes, and it's okay. So a slipstream writer can take the piss out of slipstream, because if I'm any sort of writer I'm a slipstream writer."

So what about other slipstream writers and their works? What are the roots of the movement? William Burroughs' 1983 novel *Cities of the Red Night*, with its multitude of different styles, genre hopping and surreal meta-fictional plotting, has been cited by some as an ur-slipstream work. And, more recently, Nicholas Royle's debut novel *Counterparts*, which uses distorted and skewed reality to poetic effect, has already become something of a benchmark of extended slipstream fiction. How does Allen see himself in relation to these other writers?

"I'm a great fan of William Burroughs. I wanted to get the

freedom that he has in his work, and the freedom that a lot of authors that I admire have in their work, rather than always being stuck with writing to a formula… The things he tries… he will throw anything in – he'll throw in the ingredients of a packet of tablets, he'll throw in an advert, and he'll throw in something he'd found in the street, and somehow he will get it to work within the context of the story. And that sort of freedom is the freedom I've looked for in '*The Planet Suite*', so I'll throw in horoscopes, I'll throw in handbills – anything I can think of that will help advance the story…

"How I see it is that the influences on me or any author are absolutely wild. We have instantaneous global communication, so you can be influenced by anything that's happening across the planet – any idea that's been expressed can come into your work. So things like music videos, news stories, science ideas, *Fortean Times*, anything can impinge upon your work, and the real skill is making that meaningful and entertaining."

Is there a slipstream 'movement' as such?

"Everybody's view of slipstream is like everybody's view of Science Fiction. Some count Mr X in and some count Mr X out… Slipstream is a term that people are using, so maybe there is something of a movement… If it brings me money then yes I'm part of the slipstream movement. If it holds back my career then *no* I don't write that!

"So is there a movement? Well if there is, then in this country it crystallises around THE THIRD ALTERNATIVE, and it probably includes writers like me, like Nick Royle, like Chris Kenworthy, like Rhys Hughes, and other authors I've forgotten… If there is a slipstream movement then yes I'm part of it. Whether it's a *real* movement is another matter." So after completing a slipstream novel, what's next for Allen Ashley? He mentions a novella he has in mind to write, but mainly he's concentrating on what still remains his favourite form: the short story.

"I'm not naturally a novelist. My natural forte is short stories, and – believe it or not – song lyrics… having been a failed pop singer."

He laughs at this description of himself, then goes on to lament the general low esteem in which the short story is held in professional publishing.

"I find it the cruellest irony that we live in the society of the sound-bite where people want things very succinct, easily accessible, something you can swallow straight away, and yet book publishing seems to have gone in the opposite direction – towards house bricks. You're nobody unless you're sending in a manuscript that's 800 pages long and has got two sequels. Publishers are publishing these immensely long books and don't want to know about short stories. And I love the buzz of a good short story; I love the purity of having one really good idea and exploring it..."

He becomes more animated at this point, getting into an area that excites him.

"I look for the purity of poetry in a short story – I'm not saying I achieve it; I'm not big-headed enough to suggest that. In a poem you can't have even one wasted comma let alone one wasted word, and I will try to achieve the same effect in a short story."

In *Dragon's Breath 48*, dated February 1998, noted science fiction poet Steve Sneyd responded to the interview. I normally ignore criticism but felt compelled to offer a reply, which was duly published in *Dragon's Breath 50*, dated April 1998. Both items are reprinted below – Allen

"...Ashley interview in Dragon's Breath a serendipity – someone who's an Hawkwind fan and knew of Allen Ashley re his book on the band's early years was curious what else he did, so will fire along. AA's definition of slipstream seems curiously deja vuish – would cover New Wave (or, come to that, Dada and futurist writing) – his novel gave me that, too, 'whole lotta recycling going on'. I'm all for intertextuality, but I'm happier if folk doing it seem aware that's what they're doing. Anyway – am rabbiting cattily..."
- 　Steve Sneyd, Yorks.

"I've considered this long and hard and decided that I must reply to Steve Sneyd's criticism (in D.B. 48. Feb 98). Quite *what* I've done to so upset a fellow space poet, I don't know. He suggests that I am unaware that, as is surely the case with absolutely every author since the Palaeolithic, some of my work is a re-casting and re-shuffling of earlier themes. I would respectfully point him in the direction of page 66 of *The Planet Suite*: 'There were all the films I'd seen, the books I'd read... Sometimes what I'd imagined were fresh ideas were just regurgitations'..."
- 　Allen Ashley, London

Author's Note: Happy ending and no hard feelings – I later purchased a copy of Steve Sneyd's book about Robert Calvert direct from the author.

The Almost Final Word
Introduction to the poem The Astronauts:

Ah, that lovely old chestnut that readers like to ask of writers: "Where do you get your ideas from?" Sometimes writers like to ask it of other writers or even of themselves! So, I looked back for various elements involved in the genesis of *The Planet Suite*. Where to stop? A childhood growing up exposed to the space programme. A boyhood love of science fiction – kick-started by a double pocket money purchase of *The Lost World* and *War of the Worlds*; extended by Arthur C. Clarke's *The City and The Stars* and the grand sweep of *2001: A Space Odyssey*. But soon branching out into the Earthly dystopias of Ballard and Orwell and having my young mind totally confused / being blown away by the British take on New Wave science fiction, as particularly exemplified by *New Worlds Quarterly*.

And then there was Hawkwind, around about the time of their *Space Ritual* album. A London 'underground' rock band with a stunning light show, lyrics about exploring the cosmos, fronted by a brilliant / crazed / idolised space poet, the late Robert Calvert. The course was set.

My first proper story publication came in 1982 with a horror piece *Dead To The World* in *Fantasy Tales*; reprinted several times since, including in my second collection *Urban Fantastic* (Crowswing Books, 2006). In the mid-eighties, I was briefly fronting a rock band, running a regular cabaret and trying to make a name as a 'performance poet'. My central work was a sequence called *The Space Cycle*, several sections of which I later revived in a brief 'comeback' in the late eighties / early nineties. The following poem *The Astronauts* contains the germ of a couple of key ideas that would later underpin the tales that make up *The Planet Suite*. The intertwining of astronomical and terrestrial themes – 'The astronauts are here on Earth' – is also crucial to the novel. I don't claim to have been wholly original over this – I can remember a quote from Hawkwind's Nik Turner back in an old 'New Musical Express' along the lines of, " '*In Search of Space*' was really just about us trying to find somewhere to live."

So, here's *The Astronauts*: Written circa late 1984 / early 1985; performed live with Hawkwind at The Town & Country Club (now The Forum) Kentish Town, London, December 1988; published in *Hawkfrendz Winter 88* in February 1989. For those of you with a further interest in this area, you might like to try my chapbook *Hawkwind – The Golden Void* (Hawkfrendz, 1991). For now, I'll finally do what authors ought to do: shut up and let the work speak for itself.

Thanks for reading,

Allen

(London, 2012)

The Astronauts

The astronauts are here on Earth:
their spaceship is an armoured car
in a landscape increasingly lunar.
I've seen them on the Northern sands
with Geiger counters in their hands;
their movements slowed by gravity
and bureaucratic necessity.
How the minds within the helmets
must be filled with sad regrets
for the days of weightlessness:
a heady time before ballistics
and falsification of field statistics.

Imagination leads us on –
It's *one small step* for the likes of me;
and yet, in fickle reality,
the first space age has come and gone.
We reached a psychic barrier
A hand
Maybe a mirror
which told us go no further.
Besides, considerations fiscal
so swiftly severed our umbilical;
we turned our backs on galaxies,
we changed NASA priorities

to fit in with the military's –
launching Star Wars technology
co-existent with satellite TV,
we followed the lead of Hollywood,
tail firmly wagging the dog.

You and I are parasites
we have the anti-Midas touch
turning everything to dust.
We are the poisons and disease,
there is no magic cure for these.
Boxed deposits in sea and soil
outlast Humankind itself.
Like cats we bury our detritus –
we have brought the craters back home with us
and the astronauts are here on Earth.

The watching stars turn in their courses
and secretly they must be pleased
that our abuse of Earth's resources
has kept us tethered on a leash.
Indeed, we seek the new direction
of surreptitious civil protection:
cover up the ruination,
cover up the devastation,
fill the craters beneath our feet,
trust in the highly trained elite
to do their duty and be discreet.

– And yet the world's growing hostility
reminds them all nostalgically
of a blue and white fragility
once beholden by the eyes
of a flying squad that no longer flies,
whose outward trek has been reversed…
and the astronauts are here on Earth.